The critics on Steve Aylett

'Steve Aylett is withou
ambitious and talented
England in recent year
the best of William Burr ... it has the mark of
real originality. It's hip, cool and eloquent. It's what Tom Wolfe would like to be. Aylett does effortlessly what others labour to achieve. He has a cold, accurate eye, a mocking wit and a black, playful angle of attack which has learned something from cyberpunk but has that smack of idiosyncracy, that sense of exploring new territories, that laconic, confident humour which tells you that this is exactly the book you've been waiting for. Snap it up now. Before it snaps you'
Michael Moorcock

'Wickedly funny futuristic pulp thriller: James Ellroy meets Terry Pratchett in cyberspace. The crime novel of the future, or a virtual reality instruction manual? As far away from Agatha Christie as you can go' *Daily Telegraph*

'Comic-book imagery – like Jim Steranko on steroids – mingles with a noiriste's worst nightmare . . . Distressingly brilliant' *Guardian*

'Steve Aylett knows gumshoe future-slang like Irvine Welsh knows swearwords. Initially his fast, culturally referential style leaves you gasping for air . . . but dive in and you'll be dragged along . . . a terrific read, full of armoury-loving cops, dimension-travelling robbers and the pursuit of a precious totemic book. Like Dashiell Hammett scripting a story for *2000 AD* space-girl Halo Jones, this is sci-fi for non-geeks'
The Face

'Aylett's prose is like poetry' *Independent*

'Prodigiously paranoid routines delivered with a toxic fizz. A catalogue of synapse-scorching similes any bankrupt Martian poet would kill for. Watch them scatter like buckshot through the works of all self-respecting thieves and plagiarists' Iain Sinclair

'A dizzying psychedelic rush' *The Times*

'Writes like a man possessed by comic demons . . . the pages pop in your hands like firecrackers' *Evening Standard*

Steve Aylett was born in 1967. He is the author of *The Crime Studio, Bigot Hall* and *Slaughtermatic* and was a Philip K. Dick Award nominee. If he were any more English he'd be dead.

THE INFLATABLE VOLUNTEER

STEVE AYLETT

INDIGO

Shake well before opening

An Indigo paperback
First published in Great Britain by Phoenix House in 1999
This paperback edition published in 2000 by Indigo,
an imprint of Orion Books Ltd,
Orion House, 5 Upper St Martin's Lane, London WC2H 9EA

A CIP catalogue record for this book is available from the British Library.

ISBN 0 575 40265 2

Printed in Great Britain by
The Guernsey Press Co. Ltd., Guernsey, Channel Islands

'This isn't a detonator!' shouted Irwin appalled, having tortuously dismantled the grape.

'Not as you understand it,' the Professor whispered.

Elly Rope, *Trickster's Backfire*

Contents

Eddie

A street thronging with grave-fillers.

'One false move and your guts unspool to the floor is that right.'

'Pardon me Eddie?'

'Just don't move a muscle you bastard and hand over the cash.'

'Eddie it's me.'

'Eh? Oh.'

'What are you feeling the pull to do now Eddie? And in that jacket?'

'It's a bad jacket I'll admit brother.'

'What's with the knife?'

'A precaution brother.'

'Against the cold I suppose.'

'Ah you've got me there – against the cold yes.'

'For all that's holy Eddie. Follow the rest of mankind to the bar now and begin making a sense someone can understand.'

'I will brother. I'm sorry. Yes I will and – and no jokes eh?'

The cigarette smoke had expanded to the exact size and

shape of the bar. People made of meat sat at tables made of wood. There was an open fireplace above which a wheezing rubber belly bulged and deflated as though a fat man was bricked into the flue. People came for miles to understand why it was done and who had the notion. It was nothing to do with me.

On the wall hung ornamental trilobites which would fiddle their legs when it was time to go.

'Counting coppers in a gale-strafed shed Eddie – there's your future.'

'No.'

'Only the furniture to keep you warm.'

'Not me.'

'Oh yes,' I assured him, drinking and settling down. I glanced about me and considered all I could do here with a match and a scrap of courage. 'You couldn't be serious about opening a bait shop Eddie, you see possibilities in it?'

'I had you in mind.'

'In a way that can be understood by a sane man?'

'In a way understandable to all.'

'Is it for the fun of killing small grubs which are defenceless Eddie?'

'It is, to tell the truth.'

'The day you tell the truth I'll be assuming my true form in a municipal cemetery.'

I'll explain here that friends had always held a terror for me due to my considering what colour their innards might be. Wouldn't it be terrible if they were violet and white, or blue and yellow, or all of these? Drinking with Eddie was a cheap enough distraction. Gnarly nights staggering baffled who'd sewn the bushes together.

Of course if I dropped dead Eddie would have been first

to steal my hair, the ideas at their root, my clothing, money, women, music, words and reputation. Then he'd start saying I did the murders. Then it would be dog-rogering practices and the poisoning of badgers he would charge me with as I lay cross-armed in the ruffled silk. Praying at the dark far rear of his head my eyes don't spring open and my purpling mouth demand the evidence.

Eddie himself didn't know he was possessed until his teeth were punched out from the inside. Unnecessary mess – drama for its own sake. We'd both of us had too many dealings with John Satan to be appalled but some kind of dire warning was now gathering momentum behind my throbbing forehead.

'Eddie you simple fool,' I said, 'don't you understand what that teeth scenario was meant to imply? Hell and damnation in the ancient style?'

'Hell? But a man like me would be instantly toasted.'

'That's what I mean.'

'I'll be unrecognisable.'

'Isn't that a boon after your crimes?'

'Don't know what you mean. My bones'll lock for starters – from both the fear and the constrictions of the venue.'

'I'm telling you that.'

'So what to do brother?'

'Seek to overwhelm others with your foreknowledge. Tell them you've been there before and nothing surprises you. Talk about the decor, the colour of the flames. Light your fags off the firelake. Whistle in the dark Eddie, it helps them find you.'

Eddie watched the flame-reflections on his glass a while, his expression foreshadowing by a question he'd regret.

'You've been promising for years now to give me the full

facts of how you made a pact with the forces of evil. Was it by means of an advert for those seeking love and companionship by any chance? And how does it tie in with the election and those things you were growing and Minotaur and all that business with your girl and the veins?'

'Well Eddie if you don't mind being here a while I'll explain things you never thought needed explaining.'

'Because there's stuff about Bob and so on I don't understand.'

'If you let me clarify it in my own sweet way is it a deal?'

'It is.'

'Right then.'

'None of your games like.'

'Are you quite ready now.'

'Yes.'

'Sitting tight.'

'I am.'

'Well then.'

What I told Eddie

Bone midnight Eddie – the little red lizard curled up in a rose. Yeah there's nightmares and nightmares – you know what I'm saying. I've taken part in some where the curtains have caught fire off the devil's roll-up and the clueless bastard ghosts have barged in late and we were all of us shuffling apologies to the poor sod on whom we were meant to be slamming the frighteners. Torment's not what it was. Subjective bargaining and the bellyflop of the old smarts flung a spanner in the works an age ago Eddie. That and lack of imagination. Nothing like a spider in the mouth to get you thinking.

But everything went up a notch when I met Minotaur. Bob introduced us, you know how he is. Took me to the Shop o' Fury. Whispered 'Familiarise yourself with the exit' and shoved me in. 'Want you to meet someone. No end of friends but gets through the embalming fluid, know what I mean. Crowded cellar, bare lightbulb, table, places set, rotting food, waxen faces.'

'I beg your pardon.'

'You're a man of the world brother – you know.'

'I . . .'

'Brother, meet Minotaur Babs.'

'Er . . . how do you do.'

'So this is the one. You didn't exaggerate. So, my new friend, what do you care for my establishment?'

All I could perceive was that his domain exited on to a crude skull burrow, smoking with accidents.

'A shop might be corrupt but . . .'

'I know I know,' he said, but stopped so that I wasn't sure he did. And when my eyes became true to the dark I finally had my opinion. That place had everything. Kile water. Spine dust. A pie containing an embryonic core creature – eat it and one of those apparatus would push out, stretching your scream. I felt like a kid in a candy store.

'Are these skin stitches likely to block a plughole?'

Once again I'd asked the wrong question. They were staring as if I'd punched a gran.

What's the point of it all? I thought.

'Forming in the mirror,' said Minotaur, pointing at my reflection in the very same betsy glass I'd later use to bring a demon through for the Mayor's campaign.

I got involved with that because of an enormous spider which filled my kennel and drained my good intentions through an etheric aura pump invisible to all but myself. The sinister activities of this bug excused my every offensive act but still it scared the bejesus out of me. I thought getting into politics would neutralise any goodness I harboured and starve the parasite, leaving it weak and vulnerable to assault. After the campaign I hacked an axe through the kennel roof and split the bug's thorax, which rustled like a dry seedpod – the thing had been dead for years.

In fact when I showed people the carcass they claimed there was nothing there at all. I'm surrounded by jokers.

Lazy and senior, the Mayor was a gabbing, hollow bastard whose function was to shorten the distance between the start and finish of endurance, and inevitably there were murders. Eleven, if you believe the papers. And smashing windows if you believe me – I was there when a young clerk's nerve snapped and he began shaking like a sign in a storm, bagging a vision of the Mayor with bugging eyes, and ran at him with his hands outstretched to receive the Mayor's throat for the purposes of strangulation and, later, punching. The Mayor, by now used to this and prepared, opened a small drawer, removed a gun and shot wide, hitting a small chrome effigy of a music-hall tart. The clerk tripped on the carpet, hit a window and went through, carrying with him a vase which had been on the sill. His skull broke like the vase and the vase broke like his skull, and both burst forth water mainly, and from the vase some flowers. If I could choose a death I'd make it something like that, except I'd add a good woman and some lard.

'So tell me,' I asked the Mayor later on. 'What's your secret for successful negotiation?'

'Well I invest a small hatchling core creature with the idea I wish to impress upon a person, then throw it at that person's face in the middle of a conversation. It digs soundless through ruined eyes, pulling its after-tail and unfurling an umbrella skullnest fairly quickly.'

'Aren't there drawbacks to the method?'

'A few, of course. Old brains rattle like blown eggs, victims shudder in chairs with caved faces, moving abandoned jawbones like a visor.'

'Don't you find the whole thing distasteful?'

'Swallowed muscles must live.'

'I suppose so.'

He was running his campaign on the 'raise the reeking dead' platform. The dead and silent wanted to come back, he said, they felt they'd been forgotten and the workers owed them salvation. I told him about the mirror and my ability to drag shriekers out of infernal hibernation on to the carpet like the bloody newborn.

'You propose to bring demons in here.'

'Absolutely.'

'To work.'

'What could be more appropriate?'

'Demons.'

'Yes demons. That's the song isn't it? Raise the reeking dead?'

'Yes but. We gave them tombs and memory didn't we? Names against loneliness, what else do they want?'

'Oh now it all comes out. True colours, I get it. Flap a practicality in your slack face you're backpedalling to beat the band. Do you want to deliver ghouls and revenants or don't you? It'd demonstrate your point beyond all repair like.'

'I'll. I'll have to think about this, I need time.'

'Why, to put on your thinking dress?'

Again and again shoving me with a kind of bailing instrument, the Mayor tried to move me off his desk and I shouted – don't remember what now – but only enough to frighten him a bit. Voles started abandoning the desk like rats from a sinking ship – out of the drawers and undercupboard – and the Mayor ran out of the room covering his grimace. Ill with anger I suppose.

Monsters hadn't a thing on that bastard. Black eyeballs

and flickknife ears, standing in the right place to cast a shadow, you know what I mean.

The glare of the Mayor's campaign was painful to look at directly. Here are the main points in his manifesto:

1. Wooden skulls don't work for long.
2. If we accept for the moment that reptiles have a way of knowing their own smooth charm, should we trouble ourselves with any other question?
3. Two cans of doubt and I'm anyone.
4. Bones from polar bears make grand mallets.
5. From space this Earth is incandescent with abominations – the gods write their signature in our entrails.
6. Life is much more pleasing by the standards of others.
7. Clamping those big eyes? Notify us a week ahead.
8. The main thing which has remained with me to this day is the way a severed head will become bleak when dropped underwater. A film of air will cover it to no avail. There's a lesson in that.
9. I raise my glass to rage – too pious and the stones hurl.
10. Multitudes here we go.

The opposition was a frail barber hoping to win on the 'whisper when distant' ticket. The Mayor insisted on someone making this man 'disappear'. Nobody but me knew what he meant, so I had to tell everyone the Mayor wanted him to disappear 'into the land of the dead'. What with the difficulty in getting everyone in the same place at the same time I decided to get organised and make the announcement on television. That bit of foolishness set the campaign back a full week. During that time the barber developed a tragic rapport with an oncoming truck and the Mayor laughed the big laugh.

Finally me and Bob took the mirror to the rindwoods at night and ripped the piss out of the Mayor for being scared and fronting off. 'I suppose sap is mandatory in these trees?' he asked as we trod through the dark.

'Don't make us cross,' I said, stopping abruptly – though he never noticed. Seven engines were thrumming in the centre of the forest, running the harvest and dead years. The prow of nature needed a shove these days. We laid the mirror over the old well mouth and lit a few fires.

'Ditch the cigar and read this crap Mayor.' Bob handed him a scrap of paper.

The Mayor read it out, portentous and frowning. 'The worm of the umbilical snip, head and tail subsisting – oh my brothers, that one could die. Something grows from bud to flower in darkness and fades knowing only itself. A key and a strangler – this is all a simple tale requires. Nose smuggled into the kitchen, every social custom defied.'

By now the mirror was a doorway bright with hurricane light, pouring moments over the rim in a howl of nuclear wind. A rudimentary fiend was clambering through, its form eaten down by the glare – behind it were glimpses of tolling spars, old nightropes and windlass cables bridging remains with the creak of stretched evil.

Of course the ghost was that of the murdered barber, being the latest one in. Had to cram the bastard back again, using a broom as a plunger.

Got another one out through a deeper channel, older and wiser – name of Ken.

It was all coming together. The truth was whatever you could put up with while my hands came out suddenly and punched you two at a time, not to be stopped.

In other words, anything.

The Mayor instructed everyone at the office to administer ink to a million cats – even the black ones. Nobody dared waste time telling him we planned to ignore the order – every time he raised his face we tensed for the euphoria of disobedience. Houses sank in the mush of his reasoning and that's the way we liked it. Nuns would run shrieking, but as far as I can tell that's all they're for.

Bob was instantly repentant at his part in the scam. Glared at me in the bar, growing his beard a little more. Everything in the world seemed to stop as it grew – it took that much energy. 'Flush in the sun eh?' he rumbled. 'A spear'll puncture your pear-base belly brother.'

'Will it now.'

'Neighbours processed to believe doodles.'

'What's flotsam but the measure of a land's effect on its people Bob?'

'I'd tell you what else if I felt you were ready to hear.'

'I'm ready for any wisdom *you* believe you possess.'

'Not you brother – and take that smile off your face before I smack it off and it lands slap on the portrait of Our Saviour over there.'

'That's a picture of me Bob.'

'You can finish my pint brother – I'm late for an appointment.'

When it was time for the Mayor to give a speech he took out the wrong bit of paper. 'The worm of the umbilical snip,' he began and pretty soon revenants poured out of every reflective surface, including the Mayor's reading glasses.

'You consider *this* a campaign winner?' he shouted at me from the gore-hung podium, his sparse hair flagging in the winds of hell.

'I've seen worse.'

'But the contradictions.'

'So what.'

'So what you bastard? The contradictions I said. D'you speak English? D'you know what you've done?'

'What *I've* done?'

'Yes, yes.'

'Nothing to do with me, granddad,' I said as he was swept aside by mayhem.

Ice soon scabbed over the Mayor's guilt and we thought nothing of skating on it – or on anything. 'You cannot ice-skate and be bewildered at the same time brother,' Bob rumbled. 'Try it and make me a liar.'

'It won't take that to make you a liar,' I remarked. I was poised to fall asleep when a smack in the mouth reclaimed my attention.

That's Bob for you. He now had the daunting task of peeling all the skin from his body. 'Thank heaven I'm not a heavier man,' he told me, laughing. 'Or it would take a week.'

But why had the Mayor objected to the ghost idea so much in the beginning? It's become accepted very quickly that a decomposing fiend can aid in that kind of hype but as recently as that ghosts were sort of ignored. Had a failing nobody wanted to confront – no sense of smell apparently and that marked them out. Had a hell of a time convincing the Mayor after the barber fiasco – but the other fella shrieked like a good 'un out of the roof-bugle on that van. Not about the election, but some sort of hell and torture nonsense – concentrated a lot on eyes and blood, if I recall. Death was just the start, it said. Anyway the Mayor was re-elected and we were all quite upset when the revenant pissed on the floor and said this expressed what he thought of us and our approach – slapped on a hat and left for Africa, of all places.

Of course it fell to old muggins here to categorically deny everything at a press conference amid the flashbulbs and all – you can guess what I told them.

What I told the press

Good evening – let me start by saying you can hide nothing from my all-seeing eye. Not even you sir, with your stupid vest. Or you there, with your lust for murder. Look at the heatwarp of cowardice roaring off every bastard here. My advice? A bed made of steak and a flower from the brow of a hen – establish these and you're well on the red road to the laughing academy.

But if you don't happen to have those things, form a giant lava in a cupboard – the airing cupboard, say – and make it pouch out like a bladdersack, breathing, heaving and steaming like a thing full of long-suppressed rage and straining to burst out finally in retribution and bone-splintering carnage. This mucus-glistened organ will sometimes quiver but don't let it worry you, that's just its way of showing its love. Cart it out and throw it on the bonfire when it's taller than you. That's all there is to it – and the smoke will be yellow.

But I know you're all creaming yourselves to know about the Mayor and his madness.

I can tell you the campaign glories were funded by the cartel and its leatherwinged demigod, which unfurled itself from a cabinet during boardroom meetings and silenced those who'd speak drily of statistics. Gloves and hoods, ropes in the briefcase, that sort of thing. Homoerotic rituals and enforced suicide if you reveal how boring it all is. But Skinwing had a private life when not presiding over this dour executive gloom – one that'd separate your face and your expression. He'd occasionally settle down in a pinkwall cottage to paint sleds and fishing fools and snared fish and apples and wicker baskets in one-way sunlight with the gleam on the apple just so. Nuns and rangers and strange galloshered boatmen would queue up to be copied on to canvas with their bones stuck out all angles – why he never sold the stuff's a mystery but everyone thought he would. When their heads cleared they set light to him while he slept – he rose up like a falcon and bit someone so hard they shouted with a piece took out of them like a biscuit snap.

Black with soot, Skinwing admitted everything including how he planned to duff up the grocer till dead. I admired him for that. The only time I had a crack at offing the grocer was when I saw him walking in front of a car and urged the driver to make it snappy. There's the measure of my skill in that area.

Biting enemies seems to be acceptable in a surprisingly narrow range of circumstances, or so a ninja shouted at me once. So clearly Skinners had his flaws. Larks are the same – beautiful wings but no ear for music. I knew someone who shot them on sight. 'Tigers' he called them, and shot them quickly, screaming the whole time. Fell into the large gap next to a mountain eventually. Found his bones and face picked persil-white in a holly bush, and so didn't reach in. You can't be getting torn up retrieving colleagues from the mayhem of their recklessness. Because that's what it was of course – sheer bloody-minded recklessness on his part. Even left me a sack of dung in his will.

Which got me thinking of my father's doctor as he slammed the sickroom door, my mother darting at him frantic. 'How is he doctor?'

'Dead as a doornail.'

'Stone dead?'

'As a dodo – better bury him quick.'

'Did he suffer much?'

'He made me suffer – that's enough. With the most appalling practical jokes. Throwing the medicine, that sort of thing.'

'He must have been distraught.'

'That's not the half of it, he was barking mad as a hare at the last. Pointing at Caesar.'

And I crept in to find my father with pennies on his eyes – and looking closer I saw they were made of foil-covered chocolate. Of course I stole and ate them. Magical guilt? Tell me about it.

Older and recalling this I naturally ran at once to the bar, folding myself over it and asking for something to cry about. They told me they'd give me that, and soon enough Eddie started to claim he was a roaring boy. He'd take apples and roll them along the floor, saying it proved he was a troublemaker. His latest cash cow was the 'steel underpants for bears' idea. Think about that. Bears. Underpants. Steel. I asked him how he'd advertise it and he said he'd 'create' a poster of himself putting a pair of steel underpants on to a grizzly. He said the ad would play off the mutual apprehension of himself and the bear during the procedure. And that's all she wrote.

'Eddie,' I told him in the snug, 'you're as slow as a tortoise humping a hardhat.'

Why did that bastard feel the need to stand and announce that evil was beauty, beauty evil? The whole bar fell silent and thus I myself became audible in a corner, relating the time I'd strangled a badger. My attempts to run played merry hell with the tables and chairs, people and bottles which stood so stubbornly in my way. I'd like to pretend I can laugh about it now but the truth is I laughed more then than today.

So I had to bluff it. 'Hens scream when they lay eggs,' I told them, edging toward the door, 'but it takes a finely tuned ear to hear that quality in their noises – in fact hens are screaming constantly, if we only care enough to translate them.' And I was saying goodbye solely by means of my legs.

But not everything round here's high drama. Ancient dangers are none the less dangerous. The element of surprise is available to those who either appear suddenly or have always been there. Thus the shock on the gran's face when the ancient boulder fell. The incident provided talk for a full five minutes, and then songs for ten. We boomed as though charm and a lusty aspect were enough to keep our fears at bay – and for a moment they were.

Then there was the time Eddie was savaged by saints. During the procedure these saints couldn't stop laughing and this was the main thing he recalled about the incident. 'How could they not stop?' he asked time and again, frowning at the memory. 'What am I, a comedian?'

'Nobody can decide that for you Eddie.'

'Well am I?'

'Patience.'

So that should show the general level of shiftiness we're dealing with. The shunt-thud of blade to block's the nearest you'll get around here to a square shoulder or the nod of a head. Fashion and lawnmowers come out shining and everyone tightens their fists. Apart from stamping on the animals that grow in bushes and feel it's their right to appear on the path, there's nothing to occupy us. And I mean nothing. Not even a shooting gallery with silhouettes of the royals. Put an ad in the paper once: 'Upset by fiends? Shrieking fogs speed through the room? What do you expect?' Not one reply.

Take Bob, now – there's a man who knows which side of the world his toast's buttered on and shrieks about it in the streets. Got a trick of magic which means he can call you from behind and you turn and just keep on turning, spinning like a bastard till exhaustion and insanity drain your head and structure. I like a man who can make his presence known. Nothing bloody provides a lesson for children – but call it a sauce and you'll have them screaming.

When I was a kid the devout sang a chorus of subordination and villains wore masks to keep off the glare of our envy. Born into a din of admonitions and yelling at the inconvenience, I was cruelly allowed not to know the half of it. Siblings were all over me, more boldly than spiders, dust or skin. I remember my aunt grew bonces in the garden, hid among the rockery – but there was never full development. You could stamp on them and not feel over-guilty.

What I grew best were the hydra-heads of resentment, which I fed and sang to every day. The only people who appreciated my skill were trolls, whose opinions I therefore decided to respect. I thought things couldn't get any worse – that's how young I was.

Ambition was never my strong point, and by the time I

was an adult I'd deserted the normal channels of investigation which led others to decide which consolation they wished to demand from the mistake of this dry world. For my part I wanted nothing more than to grow small heads like my aunt, and cook them to ash and sell them, as ash-heads. I tried over the years to sell this idea of ash-heads to businessmen in high glass office towers but when I came to the critical point in my pitch their expression would alter completely. Nameless men would put me on to the street and continue to hold me down as if they feared I would otherwise float away. And afterward, looking up, I would see the executive staring down at me from the twentieth floor, his expression a concentrated dot of incredulity.

Then there were the talking apes I grew in the cellar of Eddie's place – they told me everything I needed to know about apes, sand, cars, death, cheap hotels, ferns, hate, fear, hail, flamelike love and betting nags. A dossier, it turned out, was the source of their knowledge, kept in a cabinet – that's why they asked me to leave a moment, after I asked them a question, and when I returned they knew it all and were eager and precise. Annoyingly precise, as it turned out – I couldn't stand them and their smug bastard attitude. It got so I couldn't bear to feed them and they went berserk, breaking out of the depths and inflicting wounds before I'd properly awoken. And to think in the past I'd cast around looking for a horror worthy of my attention. Breaking the law to that end. Careful what you wish for brothers – it may come a-shrieking out of the bloody night with a curling lip and perfect teeth, making you know what you've done to deserve it.

'Nothing ever happens in that cellar,' Eddie declared.

'What about the wounds, the belligerence of those

chimps Eddie? Are you sailing into the port of my life and telling me that's not enough?'

But Eddie closed his eyes in a way which suggested he cared to see no other possibility.

Merging with Eddie on the furnace deal was the worst mistake of my life. He described everything as a daring speculation so why did I consider this madness any different? He described his own dull trousers as a daring speculation. His capacity for self-delusion burnt me.

Ghosts were involved in the enterprise but only because they could wraith around the oven door and make it look like cooking-smoke without us using energy for food during the baking process. In fact that was the lynchpin of the whole deal. How could I be such a fool?

So I got a job making wreaths. But I made them out of ears and was arrested after only four days. In that time I'd sold nine hundred wreaths at a profit of £560. Which I wasn't allowed to keep of course, it being defined as 'illegal earnings'.

And that's the last job I had before getting into that shitstorm of controversy with the Mayor and all. Went for an interview last week as any poor sod could see the ship was sinking and the bloke asked why I hadn't looked for a proper job in years. So I turned on the old waterworks and said last time I'd considered the idea all hell broke loose in me head. 'I shamed myself quite frankly,' I said. 'Learning things I already knew and wasting years on the process. Last time there was a dog in the way – nothing more but I used that as my excuse not to proceed. Well in fact there was no dog – that's how uncommitted I was. But I said there was a dog. I can't repent enough.'

'There's nothing on your CV regarding hobbies,' he said.

'Well I crave abomination and so attempt to invoke the devil in my free moments. With varying degrees of success, of course.'

'I beg your pardon?'

'The devil. I invoke him. Summon him up as it were. Surely you've heard of this.'

'Heard of it. Yes, I have.'

'Well there you are. And I've gained some measure of notoriety by my efforts.'

'I'm sure. Yes I.'

'Yes. Well is there anything else you needed to know? Tell you what, I'll explain my position, all right? It's a maze of sickness and blunder, now that I think about it – but I see where to begin.'

What I told the interviewer

Roadkill intercourse – yes, those precious obstacles are the main event in my life and it's a form of love so obscure nobody's ever reviled my activities or dragged me into the hay-strewn square for the purpose of flogging amid toothless hags and free-range poultry. I'm thankful for that and for a clear understanding of my good fortune, because a lot of bastards in this world don't know when they're getting away with a good thing.

This was years after my bust-up with Rube, who had hair like the silk off a sweetcorn and a brain like the sweetcorn itself, multiple-sectioned and each section running a different personality. Her arse was poised precisely one and a half miles above sea level.

Nobody approved, least of all Bob. 'Ruby's a scorched-earth murdering bitch surely. Those stitches down the middle of her face.'

'She had an accident.'

'Stop laughing at least. God Almighty.'

Barbs were hurled at me as mere words of condemnation and slander are hurled at common men – and I collected them all in my back like a porcupine. Because that's the kind of cowards these bastards were – no sooner had I turned away than they were carefully considering what I'd said and done. As if it were jaded knowledge I dealt in hundred-horsepower bullshit.

We were once sat having a meal in a smoking ruin. A masterpiece of arson actually, produced out of a nearby cathedral – went along to spectate the black Atlantis of its remains. Charcoal and coloured glass – I felt no more blessed amid this mess than amid the original construction, and there's a lesson in that. We were discussing Ruby and defence, and Empty Fred said he'd left his trousers in a hero-guarded shrine at the end of the universe.

Eddie remarked that this was rare and unfortunate.

'Eddie it happens all the time,' sighed Fred witheringly.

'Not you though Eddie,' I stated. 'You'll end the low way. A skull and a few hair-wisps brother, that's the truth.'

'Ah so that's the truth is it – I can stop questing now.'

'Oh questing, is that the fresh song?'

'It is.'

'Redeeming your exploits by slamming a moral template over 'em like a sandwich toaster eh?'

Bob uncorked his soul and stood. 'When men cannot effect cannibalism, can only be judged by evils, as distant cities go quiet in collapse and trouble, I will make toast by the river, and remember the warning I gave you this day.'

'Beg pardon?'

'You heard.'

'Perhaps their hands'll go out like cigarettes,' I chipped in.

'He understands,' said Bob, pointing at me.

'Well, not really,' I said uncertainly.

'Fancy playing tennis with a spider monkey's head

anyone?' asked Empty Fred, producing one, and Bob lunged at him with his entire body.

An hour was worth an hour in those days.

Latex and bigotry was all the rage and I couldn't get enough of it, punching team players every chance I got. Thought I was blameless because of the trend – but oh the suffering and guilt I felt later when Fred told me I'd ruined his day the time I torched his car and floated a dead wren in the bath as he tried to go on holiday for the first time in years. Have a beer on me I said, and ran. Guilt's such a red pleasure.

Fred was fated to die like a hero with a missing advantage. Tumour on his uniform. I like to think if we'd known we would have all behaved differently. Minotaur visited his stable and started snogging the horses – said they wanted it as much as he did. 'Look at 'em,' he laughed, gesturing at the row of long faces. 'Batting their lashes. I'll save one for you, brother.'

'He's using each individual stable as a kissing booth,' said Fred, appalled. 'He can't tell right from wrong.'

'But I can snog with the best of 'em,' laughed Minotaur, flushed, his arm round the neck of a mare. He and the horse looked at me and this became a snapshot I'd carry through life.

Hunting was the pastime I always returned to and soon it was bears I was after, thinking they were as small as their picture in the books I had. I took with me a wicker basket in which to keep the doll-limp bodies. Suffice it to say I returned after five weeks of bleeding in the mountains and biting at rats, with a new philosophy which involved sitting in the corner of an uneventful room and saying nothing. Drawers were filled with the guns and other bastard implements I was sure I'd never use again, and there was a locked door to keep women from grabbing me. Soon I was cured even of whispering, and ladders appeared at my window surmounted by the ruddy faces of the scornful and incredulous, all a-veiled with nose-steam. Someone tied a beggar to a pole and pushed him at the upper wall, making him relay messages of support – but he was from Sweden or something, the words were repeated phonetically and you know what that means. Complete bollocks and I felt worse than ever.

A white drop of holy water exploded on my forehead like a snubnose bullet. The eyes which claim and have always claimed to belong to my head sprang open and some bastard was stood there administering the last rites and stealing a shirt. 'Three guesses,' I choked, decent and appalled, 'is more than you'll get as regards my response to this.'

Sweetness and spades kept the funeral civil. The closing earth, a white hand tucked away as an afterthought, and roses. And no memory among the locals of the holy man's visit – he had asked for this and they had prayed for it.

The sky clotted with angels.

My journal records it as such, as you can see here: 'Broke out of the straps and punched guard – watched him fall all the way down before I ran, that's how cool I was at this most desperate and extreme moment. They shouldn't have expended energy on considering that a bastard like me could stay silent that long without perking up and going on the rampage.'

And that's one of the milder entries. Search me, if you're not afraid of scorpions.

Eddie, by the way, looks like one of those mummified frogs you find in a coconut if you're lucky. From the very start we'd meet regular and discuss current affairs.

'Will they reel in surprise at the next disaster Eddie or will they learn?'

'I think they will reel in surprise.'

'Are you sure now?'

'Five of these confirm I am.'

And he counted out five coins on to the dark table. Each one sprung legs and fiddled away out of sight with a spider's swiftness.

'And just what does that really confirm,' I said into a beer, 'except that you have the red ear of the devil?'

And I fell to thinking of the eight times in my life I'd met the devil and the very particular boredom it caused me. The first time was in Eddie's gallery and the last was in Eddie's shed.

Paintings plagued that gallery.

'Get rid of 'em Eddie,' I bellowed. 'They'll bleed you dry and leave you choking in your mess.'

Eddie tried to describe the function I'd misunderstood – that they weren't here to prevail against sense and actuality. That's how far gone he was, and of course I lost no time in banging him round the face with a rolled-up hand – he fell in a corner so precisely I thought for a moment he was agreeing with my argument – then I realized he was out like a light – then the devil came. Well you know the rest.

Next day Eddie said he'd leap off a building and naturally I spectated from below but a shower of birds, monkeys and cats descended instead of that lying bastard. Some dead before and all dead after. The birds in particular had been strangled and the chimps punched senseless. That's the sort of work I'm claiming he performed. And he asserted I should be 'enriched' by the experience. 'I suppose you'll want paying then,' I shouted, and when I saw his gob moving to form the affirmative I kicked it hurriedly in the other direction.

I didn't want to be lumbered with this nonsense my whole life – especially a life as short as mine was plainly to be. So I searched for a reason to leave the continent entirely, and having settled upon an excuse – demonic possession and exotic cure, if I remember correctly – I quit the land of my birth and set off in a boat made of dead wood and ignorance. Both the wood and the ignorance kept me afloat. There's a lesson I learnt early.

Bereft of the support systems of alcohol and bloody vengeance, however, I was reduced to stoning gulls and small surfacing pilchards – for two months. Built a crude effigy of Eddie which I propped in a corner of my cabin and used for the receiving of darts by the painful end. I was so bored I could have gazed at an ornament.

I swear all the terror later on was justified – blood spattered a wall but I was perfectly intact. A spider's web carried away my tears into the shadows. Footsteps without anyone riding them entered and departed.

Finally I stopped thinking I was a normal man. Looking at the facts, I felt quite comfortable with this assessment.

So anyway I arrived. And wished immediately I was back with the bastards who'd urged me I shouldn't leave in the first place.

Skulls everywhere for a kick-off – and not recognisably human. Snouted like a pike. Looked at you wherever you sat in the room, that sort of thing. Which was the last thing I needed in m'darkness, I can tell you.

Smashed them – every one with a hammer, big one that fitted over my shoulder as a hammer should. And those mothers exploded like crockery, fragments flying like the stumped notions of lazy poets. I laughed to fulfil my contribution. I hadn't eaten or thought clearly for weeks.

I salvaged a few things to be proud of in that wrecked land. Bellying out in a way that frightened the natives and made the already running ones stop suddenly and stare. Loving the sky as much as the earth, I told them so and made them know I was watching their response, oh so close. Shaking with fear, some of them. 'Ghosts,' I said – just the one word. And they were fleeing.

You'd think this paradise of billowing delirium could last forever, but it did end one spring morning. I was having a sparse picnic under a varicose tree. Ratcheting a new trap, I laid it down and hoped I'd catch something bigger than an actor this time. Eleven minutes later I had concrete proof that some spiders have enough meat to throw the mechanism – this one was so heavy it started shouting as I picked it up, claiming I shouldn't waste time trying. I must say I agreed. This bastard looked intent on being a dead weight, giving me not a bit of help. And could anyone hope to fry it into a meal worth the crunching?'

Renewed and wily, I came home glowing like a dashboard saint. Bearded and staring. Built a building flighty and ramped, soldered with cheese, scabby with windows, nothing its number, guilt its foundation. A cabin in a hill, inset like an eye from which I could survey louts as they went their way screaming and holding hands. Sailing kites which they thought were fun and blameless, but which I knew and sometimes informed them were inadvertent signals to the devil himself. Hot scenes would ensue and I'd have to run like the clappers because they supposedly knew it all. Nothing ever entertained people as much as me – not even circus acrobats who fell just so when shot in mid-air. Only the elephants seemed to find it amusing like I did. Just me and the elephants.

Went back the other week – heard it had been turned into a school for midgets and wanted to see. Nothing had changed except it looked bigger.

So I was stood savouring my past when someone came up and punched me eighty times on the front of my face. 'But try lunching on it,' I said nervously, trying to be a lad. Next thing I remember is the doctors telling me I was lucky to be alive. 'You mean I'm intact for indoctrination?' I sneered, and was still sneering when they pushed me out the doors. Well anyway, I told them. Got home and wrote a huge treatise on geese, about which I know nothing. 'It's a routine bird,' I concluded, lighting a cigar, 'I can take or leave it.'

Next day I was putting a match to a car in Epping Forest and a badger came near. 'Get away you *bloody* gobshite!'

But it was too late – everything went up and he was off calling the police. I had some explaining to do they said. A lot of explaining.

What I told the police

It all comes down to my unbeatable charm – that's the reason for everything that happened with the badger back there and so on. Don't interrupt. Just don't touch me you bastard. See this here – tattoo of a dead git. That's where we'll all be, in time. Write *that* in your book, if you can. Now where was I—

Talking to Eddie in the bar I was. 'Penny for your thoughts brother.'

'The clockwork quality of the human female bomb,' he said. 'You?'

'Shelled pride and candied anger.' At this point I necked some beer and knew I'd done so. 'I trust you've a plan.'

'Logic and temperature are joined somewhere – when I find out where, I intend to stand on it.'

'And then?'

'Explain to everyone what I'm doing.'

'Because it might just look as if you're standing idle.'

'Exactly. And you?'

'I will balance stone deities on my arse until they're all retired.'

'You'll be balancing stone deities on your arse a long time.'

'Don't count on it.'

It was a routine argument, existence adoring strife and psychic mistakes.

'An earpopping roofdive Eddie – there's your end.'

'Not me.'

'Oh, yes. Tarmac blur and a smack you'll barely register. Merciful really. Or a hanging. You'll dry all right.'

'Wrong.'

'Coleridge's deck withered his officers. Why not you? You'll change for the clock in your skin.'

'Not likely.'

'Only yesterday eyes and all, to die and unweave with the dead.'

'No.'

'Summers without pictures.'

'Never.'

'Kicking madly in a wind.'

'Nonsense.'

'Knotted witnesses.'

'Bollocks.'

'Banging tense against a gibbet.'

'You go too far brother.'

'Sacred bargains – that's the key Eddie. To your existence at any rate.'

'No deals,' said Eddie.

'Oh really,' I said unconvinced. 'And you're just unconnected with everything else then. Look at these gems Eddie – don't you feel hungry?'

'Not me.'

Eddie's bare assertion that he was above it all filled me

with a rage like boiled poison. Friends rallied round. Kill him when all his eyes are closed and his arms are in an anti-punching position. Then his death's assured. But I stared out the window and considered the effect of these negligible actions. So here was their understanding of the wiring under the boards. Bottle-brave and fronting off. Seeking to overwhelm me with impoverished paradigms I'd always dismissed as the ghoulish instinct of chefs. Changing opinions like a gator thrashing its weight.

Should I stop here and let these dime-a-dozen bastards shout pointblank into my eyes? Or go home?

New skeletons with still-oiled joints are almost soundless – old ones clatter and have poor luck when creeping up on you. Just one of the lessons I learnt in the front room of that strange house at three in the stagnant morning. Braille wallpaper, meaty flies and attic drybirds.

The room was so icy I couldn't shift the furniture.

'Is this glue or am I in the worst place I've ever been?' I asked the suicide line.

'The worst place *so far*,' they emphasised.

'I feel better,' I said – and I honestly did. There's something about fools on the line that creates perspective – what could be worse than being the other bloke?

That building was radiant with neglect. Beautiful gargoyle over the door but it started shouting at me with the spooky black hole of its mouth – saying I was ridiculous, a failure. And that within a year I'd develop gills.

Draped it in kelp. I saw seaweed as the answer to everything in those days. What a fool I was. Someone had allowed me to go that way for years and now I was seeing for myself.

So I stopped at the bar.

Through mere conversation a while back I'd caused a

previously mild cleric to become dangerously insane and as I glanced across the bar now I saw him thunderously bargaining with a pinioned victim. 'Do you care to live more?'

'Oh yes.'

'Are ye sure now?'

'Yes, yes I—'

'You do?'

'I – yes I do please.'

'Well there's wisdom. There's wisdom eh boys? Aye, they say aye. You're a small man. Small men need to remain silent or know the power of my legs.'

'Yes.'

'Yes what?'

'Yes padre.'

Preggers with grim knowledge, I turned to Eddie. 'How smallminded can a man be and remain a punching target Eddie? Just how bloody small?'

'Don't know what you mean brother.'

'You know all right – you know.'

'Not me.'

This was Eddie. The one time he tried growing a beard it turned out green. Fingered something out of his ear which struggled and scarpered – finally cornered by police in an alley and shot eleven times. Media blackout and Eddie in quarantine for six weeks – there's the sort of man he was.

'Every moron and wreck knows more than you Eddie – for example that pigs can be turned inside-out when very young, before their bones harden.'

'All bones are hard.'

'There – that's how much you know today.'

'Yes it is – and I'm right.'

'Won't admit a mistake. Doomed to failure and the

indefinite delay of anything you might enjoy, do you understand what I'm telling you? Do you get my meaning?'

'Ah you've a meaning now?'

'One I've had with me since a youth plagued by swivel-head statues and leg-dangling ceiling parasites. My God you're a babe in the woods.'

'Did you ever return home brother?'

'When my father died. The Reaper warned me in advance you know.'

'You really believe you're acquainted with him.'

'The Reaper. Didn't I take you to the very depths of hell proving the point.'

'Oh so you did. I always remember it as a kind of holiday or surgical procedure. Nearly died on the table. Pool table that is – ha ha ha.'

'Quite a joke Eddie,' I stated, and regarded my pint closely. 'Yes, quite a little joke there.'

'Oh so you liked that eh?'

'I know you've been planning it for some time – and I wouldn't knock a man in his finest hour now would I?'

'Oh I get your full meaning now – you're casting asparagus is that it?'

'I am.'

'Well that's your way, I know.'

'Each to their own Eddie, that's right.'

'Each to their own. It's the only way.'

'Hell yes it's the only way.'

'Now what were we discussing again?'

'Lard Eddie.'

'Lard. Unbeatable.'

'Oh you sad fool.'

Like I say, I could understand only so much per day

about Eddie – but Bob was a different language altogether. Charm bounced off him like rocks off a bastard. Even Ruby couldn't get him to release the hen he'd caught one time in an alleyway – and he said it was because he intended to shave it before releasing it back into the wild. '*Then* we'll see if nature takes care of its own or stamps on its face and calls it outcast,' he whispered, stroking the animal.

'Bob why interfere with the natural order of this rubbish?' I said, gesturing at the trees.

'Measured against death, weeping for a very long time can seem like a political observation.'

Ruby disagreed, saying tears were too full of nourishment for that. She'd done a whole bunch of experiments whereby a diet of tears had accelerated the regrowth of lobster arms torn off in seafloor combat.

Back in the bar Empty Fred was taking bets as to how many people could fit into the pub before they'd start evolving – he meant into a creature which hung from the ceiling by a sucker, with one arm for the pint and a gob for expelling bullshit. 'Only three,' I said, giving him a tenner, 'if they were all like you.'

Everyone froze, staring at me as if I'd committed the last and worst of a catalogue of crimes. My laughter abandoned me like a viper leaving a dry victim.

'You hear?' I bluffed nervously. 'Rotfaced discoveries in Charlie's wall – wife on long holiday indeed.'

'You're a smooth one aren't you. How do you keep from besotting us all?'

'I use a charm filter.'

At that moment the barman staggered up from below with a roasted pig on a platter, rosy flanked, apple in its gob. Thank God, I thought – a feast for distraction.

'Look what I found,' the barman shrieked. 'Bloody murder.'

'Dead – and pumped with deadly venom I daresay.'

'That's a relief,' I shouted hopefully, but was met with glares of disapproval as the whole bar gathered at the corpse.

'Some monster put it through torture before the end.'

'Look at that expression – if you can.'

'What was the cause, d'you think?'

'Auto-erotic asphyxiation,' I said. 'Look at the apple.'

'That's satsumas brother.'

'Any idea who bothered to do it Eddie?'

'Him,' said Eddie, pointing at me as though at a passing silver aeroplane. 'That murdering bastard over there. Doesn't know his own desires. Talks about the dry-tissue-clung eye sockets of dead birds. Can't keep his mouth shut about his mother. Bedroom's a front. Radar screens and illuminated continent behind a flip-up wall. There's the bastard.' And he pointed again with more emphasis on the malevolence.

A minimum of eight people said I deserved worse than they could imagine. The barman yanked up my sleeve.

'How'd you get the scar brother.'

'Brown turbulent sea, jellyfish out of nowhere, end of story.'

'End of story.' The bar reverberated with scornful laughter. 'Yeah I bet.'

'It's true.'

'Story of your life eh – end of.'

'Yeah – end of, yeah, my life er . . .'

'No story brother – no plot but the one against us, no conflict as we've no defence.'

And what did that leave me? Only a set of evasive

manoeuvres the subtlety of which would blow the ears off an adder.

What I told every last bastard in the bar

Right then lovebirds, simmer down – that's right, that's right. You're all my little babies eh? You with the knife – just you try it. And stop with the pocket billiards Eddie.

Now there's compelling reasons for realising this here isn't a pig like you say. This is a spaniel in the last stages. You'll notice the snout here is bevelled and made of cardboard, as we can all hear if I strike it. Hear that? And see the remnants of hair? The smile on its face? See the large canines? D'you even speak English? Think you're clever eh? Now I see it all. Jellied eyes broadcasting their disapproval by the energy of their belief that I care. And you seriously consider I do. Well that's your right, of course. And one smile from life forms a rope for showing where your head ends.

Truth is I'd like to light the fuse of every dog's tail and watch them shout. That's right fry the monsters till they understand how I hate. Nothing can help me to feel better so quickly as the enterprise I just described. Get frowning now you bastards, I won't change my mind.

Frown and you're using your best wares for something that truly expresses what you feel. When I do so I'm proud

I haven't given way to thoughts of light and endearment. My rule for life is to be desperate one day at a time. The roof exists only to conceal what the world is about to heap upon me. Like yesterday at Fred's we heard the ceiling creak and having squatted into a starter's-orders sprint position I felt I was way ahead of him, right. But the ceiling banged open and dumped four tons of insects on to us like a glittering rubbish heap.

Empty Fred was laughing. I was so pissed I tried wading over to punch him but he was already being overwhelmed by the brittle masses.

The insects started raising their preystick arms and throwing quivershadows on the wall. 'Their way of showing disapproval,' said Fred, choked with hilarity.

Examined a few, but I never could identify animals. Last week I was flooding the banks with saliva, slivers of gill and drifting snot, paddling hell-for-leather away from a harmless seal. Wet old hags told me I was to be king and I was so bored I dunked their heads in the cauldron. Frighten them at their own game brothers.

Making enemies is a sculptor's art, full of fury and patience. The oven should be set at gas mark bloody seven. And stand back or your eyebrows'll join your reason. Carve out the shape of a barge on a patch of land and tell 'em it's an ark plan – see the blazing rage of the devout and laugh with a roar like a lion. Sacks of spuds should be stored away because you'll have to hide for eight months. When it's all blown over you can emerge anew, take yourself off somewhere and open a small antique shop under an assumed name – they'll find you one day with a gun in your gob and a thousand incriminating relics in the attic. That's the way for a man to go, not sobbing at a crossing with a pram and spaniel, shouting your woe and blaming your foe – where's the shrapnel in that?

Infinitely more interesting to me are those who think nothing of stalking wraiths and, upon snaring one, hurl abuse at it. I find their lack of respect unsettling but their perfect boldness a tonic in m'darkness.

In short, my life's a blemish on the arse of humanity, unseen and shameful – neither tragic nor a problem under most circumstances. This has never changed, but I've learnt that a man must go where he's welcome if he wishes for conviviality, and where he's unwelcome if he wishes for mayhem and adventure.

Carp can speak – that's what I really wanted to tell you all this time. Carp can speak and the things they say are so full of justice the average man cannot contain it in his mortal frame.

Drums beat when they speak – like the primitive drums of white-robe druid ceremonies, stone circles, drizzle, smoke and steam merging till nobody knows where the hell they're standing in relation to each other. Unbeatable.

Carp may have been only pretending to speak, but to me it was real and I had evidence – that of my own senses, and camerawork of a skill rarely seen today, panavision impossibilities they refused to show at the scientific congress when I banged in during someone else's address to the scientific community's embarrassment and the sound equipment's inability to convey my wisdom when the incident was later shown in the early hours to a death squad.

I returned home a damaged man and stained by celebrity. Under the well, in a kind of siding, killer ants held a council and decided I was the man to seek for advice on their next step, as it were – we're talking here of a little-known attempt among that kingdom to slash and burn mankind before it could do the same to them. I loved their company, they were warm, convivial, honourable, and worthy of anyone's respect. Stampeded over the lawn when I called them in for dinner – played tennis and flew, sometimes. Give me an ant for that sort of mellow activity. Have one for a friend and you're set for days – which for them is a lifetime.

Nothing stopped me from reporting it at once to the media. Ignored me of course, as I should have expected. Lavish reports the next day of some fool who fell into a ditch – what's funny about that? The only time I found that interesting was when a bastard friend of mine fell into a kind of ditch years ago – I'd punched him with a sort of oriental knife I was proud of in those days – and when he fell I shouted his name in order to provide him with the last thing he'd hear this side of the Styx. It was a blistering winter and he froze there, the impersonation of Walter Matthau still on his face. This had been the cause of our disagreement and delayed his identification for a long time. I had by then left the area and blazed a trail of savvy and might across the high country.

My skeleton was hoarding blood for a prancing of its own after the death of this flesh, you know how it is. Our first breath in cells is fresh-printed currency, citizens without offence. Then the accusations. The prolonged hostaging of found cats, for tame starters. Next – failure. Then disguises fall away like onion layers and from nothing they fall. Thinkers are temporarily a fringe. Soon it's rather less temporary. Two sides to every argument and don't dare suggest a third or eighty-seventh. Till finally events pile lunatic weight on drained ambition. Every man a martyr. The steam from his guts though, to show he meant business. Justice? So explain the burnt vanguard, the rags, the cracked sadness.

You can scoff. Oh, draw knives why don't you. Can't you let good fall to good and slovenly behaviour flourish in the few corners it may? Love's weighted by so many leery bastards it's a wonder it grew in the flesh loam. Losers cram my door, unaware only two at the most can enter at a time. Juice explodes as they overstep the limit physics allows – the juice of blood and naivety.

Consider this – a man enters a barber's. Says he wants everything cut away – and I mean everything. They kick him out. Have they done what he requested? To answer that question we have to go all the way back to the fifth century. At that time my earliest traceable ancestor was a barber named Gibby who tried to make it known that shoving a dwarf first one way and then the other was not a fruitful activity, especially if you, too, were a dwarf. History has shown that his views, though scorned at the time, filtered into the mainstream. Bargains were struck whereby latex hooves were placed on sleeping waiters and they were then awoken by the loud banging of kettles and pans, at which they would stand and remove the hooves. This was the only real form of amusement in the Middle Ages. There are twelve explanations for this, each as dismal as the last. And I don't propose to waste any more time on it now.

Suffice it to say no amount of clapping could disguise Gibby's death.

So anyway after the ant débâcle I went to Carver's of all places. When I arrived Carver was moving his hands in the air as if he was holding something. Carver could waste valuable time till the cows came home. There was nothing he could do if it was important enough. I walked past the shack once and he was singing something I can't explain. I'd asked Carver what he thought 'death' was and he said it was a kind of soup. He'd somehow I think drawn up his soul and crammed the lot into his skull, leaving his body free to do what it would. No wonder there were cattle and gamblers in his kitchen, letting off steam to beat the band. People were skidding in lard round there. Nobody believes me now but I saw a short man in pure green velvet, stamping on a wren repeatedly in a dim-lit corner. He was shrieking like a major and the words he spoke were so lacking in wisdom I was sick.

'Oho Carver,' I hailed as he endeavoured to focus his eyes. 'I'm over here – by the guillotine.' Carver had a pintsize guillotine he reserved for elves.

'Oho,' he said, and that was all. I repeatedly clapped my hands to get his attention.

Once when I was trying to talk seriously to this man he fell suddenly backwards into an unused well where he underwent an epiphany of unwanted grit.

I left, swearing never to try again.

Back in town, nothing had changed. Leaping into an empty pram amid the screams of women, Eddie tried to reclaim his youth. But the pram began to roll down the street bouncing and telling him it was his punishment – in his mind, like, he heard this said to him, along with advice on furnaces and coal tar, if he's to be believed at all. Under the pavement at exactly the same time a sewer crocodile was following his course all the way, being the most exciting thing that had happened to it for two years – the last thing being the time a travelling clown was locked under the drains by an unofficial committee, who later said nothing of the matter to each other though they felt a weight of guilt occasionally in the chestal area – the croc, as I was saying, saw the sobbing clown as he tried prising open the drain hat and thrashed toward him with a grin a mile long, as the crow flies.

So what if you've heard it before?

What you don't know is the horrors in Eddie's basement – and I don't mean the apes. I was there a few weeks ago. Chains ring from the floorbolt to the wallbolt. All it needs is an Igor with a strong arm and the floorhatch lifts, belching smoke from the underlab. 'That's what's missing round here,' Eddie said, 'a real, quality hunchback for your money.'

'I can see that,' I scorned, my words reverberating in the scabby chamber. 'But why pay when you can pretend well enough you don't need a thing?' And I turned back to him at the door. 'Not that I can *now*.' And I stamped out, slamming the heavy, impenetrable door. It was another fortnight before I saw Eddie and by then he was blade-thin and furious, screaming of rats and their dry attentions.

You should see the stuff he's got growing round there. Ears. Eyes. Oh yes eyes can grow like anything else brothers – three yards is the record. Like poles of white glass, and as useless if you ask me. But fads will take their course.

Photographed the whole lab. Espionage camera concealed in my arse. Snuck off. Sniggering. Clever. One up for the reds.

Sat in the confessional, developing the film. Heard a voice from the other side of the spyhole. Requesting information. Personal. Sick. Sort of stuff I'd never tell anyone or admit to myself.

'Is this how you make your spondulicks *padre*?' I remarked, smirking in the dark. 'A man like me lives it, know what I mean?'

'How many times can a man in such misery dodge a bus?' said the mournful voice.

'It's a good question.'

What I told the priest

Our despair's so comprehensive round here it'll take more than your miracles to shift it padre. It's all very well you firing surface-to-air prayers as time robs cells from your brain and your heart breaks like a wishbone. If joy exists it's to no avail, maybe on a dead moon. False food and cups filled with concrete. There's so much trouble in the world flies ought to be praised for being small enough to ignore. Take Minotaur. 'You're just gunna have to trust me on this one Belly,' he shouted the other day, pushing the old 'dozer into gear. 'Or stand by and let the real men rule.'

'Don't call me Belly you gobshite,' I yelled, priming the rifle. 'If you think I'm about to let you ride roughshod over my life, you're putting more planning and effort into your career than I am.'

'Right again, as usual,' he remarked, and began trundling over everything.

And Eddie, who once saw fit to criticise my life and abilities. I remember it because the ornamental trilobite on the pub wall behind him was giving birth to a flood of spiders. Spreading like an inkblot on a page.

'A man always with a ready alibi eh brother?'

'Correct.'

'Rizla English and the violence to show it eh?'

'Too right Eddie.'

'Making choice remarks on the facial imperfections of others.'

'Yes.'

'Telling yarns which are structurally unsound due to their being made up as they go along.'

'If you say so.'

'Journeying by the sure aim of your fist.'

'Is there another way?'

Eddie took a long draw of the pint while keeping his eye pointed at me. Then he said:

'By God brother you're a sick one. What ya lookin at? Oh Christ shit fuck – insects!'

Bob though – now there's a scary one. He'd drawn several dozen nerves out of his chin and deliberately tangled them to resemble an ordinary beard. 'Don't you understand why I grow this?' he hissed urgently one evening in the bar.

'To blur the delineation of where your chin ends and where the atmosphere surrounding it begins.'

'No you fool look.' He prodded a finger into each eyesocket and drew off his skin like a rubber hood – the skull beneath was smoothly ribbed like a moulded jelly basin. '*Here*'s what I have to contend with all day every day.' He began pulling on the headglove again. 'The more distraction there is from this little nightmare the less crap I have to take from narrowminded bigots.'

'Did you think I didn't know about that? Wasn't I taught to know that sort of thing from my early years?'

'You mean, all this time.'

'I just said so. And did you ever take any stick from me about it? Don't I have better things to do than making fun of your head?'

'No.'

'Well, be that as it may . . .'

Went to his place once. 'By God brother it's like the eighties in here.'

'Sure it's a grey and airless wasteland of banality suffused with the impossibility of imagination or true creativity and anyone trying to grow in this'll have a time getting out with a living heart and soul and those who claim to be the way-out-and-wacky ones are as drab as the rest thus lowering the threshold of individuality to somewhere below the knee and in an atmosphere like that is it a wonder the bastards who voted for death took a decade and a half to realise the fucking obvious and who were all the cunts who thought it was a fine old time and now won't even admit they were there and for those of us with the wit to see in all its horror what we were living through it was like being awake during bloody surgery and no wonder we were offing ourselves left right and centre and now it's all retrospective and no one's responsible and what a surprise and we're all wise now well let me tell you Sonny Jim apart from a bit of music the only difference now is there's fuck-all money to be had anywhere and the song's all caring-and-sharing because after all people like to pretend they're in control of their withered lives and that they're poor and ineffectual by their own free will but I can feel the sterility of those times around the edges of my vision brother and it never goes away.'

'Exactly. Is that Eddie I hear?'

We went to the window and looked down at Eddie on his bicycle in the little yard. He was trying to give the riding of it some sort of sexual connotation. Bob threw open the window. 'Your tears'll freeze into thrones for hurricane angels Eddie.'

Eddie twisted round in surprise, and smiled. 'Oh right brother.'

'He's continuing,' I said, appalled.

Later Eddie came in for some lard and saw me at the table making a skipping rope out of a length of my gut. 'What have you and Bob been talking so much about?'

'Oh you know, the sea bubbling a tumble of skulls, forgotten clots of history resurfacing to our shame, a million years emerging, mastheads breaking the surface of the water, running the blades against a twilight sky, thoughts spilling into the sea foam and streaming from flapwind sails, that sort of thing. Eyes slamming open in the bellowing hull.'

'That room of his eh? Did you know Bob's father went to the Arctic Circle, cut his throat in an igloo which stained through like a bloodshot eyeball, then came back as a ghost to boast about it? But the wound had carried over and he couldn't speak so he had to mime the whole thing. Picture it now.'

'No.'

'Picture it a ghost now, trying to say that in gestures. Especially the bit about the stain. I can tell I'm frightening you brother. Love a good ghost story me.'

'I'll break your fucking face if you don't tell me something that's truly worth the hearing Eddie. Just once do that.'

Myself I never had a good time finding somewhere to live.

'Would you like to see the hunk of head we keep here?'

'Yes if it's an attraction certainly.'

'Oh it is,' said the landlady, and opened a wardrobe to reveal a fragment of the Statue of Liberty's face and eye, all covered in moss and shite. 'That's our pride and joy.'

'I can see why. Do you get much trouble from the police?'

'Oh no – they come round as often as the rest. These cables run through a wormhole in space and secure the entire world in position.'

She pointed at nothing at all, then shrieked down at a little drift of ropes which lay, severed, on the floor. The whole building began to subside, windows popping like soapbubbles. I was taking my leave when she grabbed my arm and shouted, 'Oh mister – we're dead, all dead.'

I've noticed this in moments of extremity – bastards barring my way and stating the obvious. Another time I was digging for spuds and hit a skull, which caved like an egg and released some sort of noxious gas. I would have dealt with it in my own sweet way if it hadn't been for some fork-leaning fatso in the next ditch saying, 'Hit a skull which has released gas eh?' Naturally I barrelled at him and within minutes was digging him in. So what could have been a curious anecdote became a cause for guilt and caution which is still with me.

A year later the potato-puppies I'd seeded began to clot that yard like white embryos. They weren't at all like the little squash-heads my aunt had taught me to grow for roasting. These things squealed at a nosebleed pitch and roiled their chubby limbs, which swelled at an alarming rate. No pigmentation in them at all. I was scared and didn't know why.

You've guessed the rest. Went out there with a spade and started denting them in, hacking splits in them and feeling sick at the purple innards. Whole lot started screaming bloody murder, biting my trouser-ends with gummy jaws and looking me bang in the eye like baby seals. No describing my disgust with myself. It's radishes from now on, I thought. A man shouldn't be reduced to tears by his hobbies.

Mind you every time I try to make a change around here I encounter greed and avarice, oh yeah. Made a huge maggot out of clay on one occasion and everyone made it memorable by dragging it out of the kitchen and setting fire to it in the road. Then everyone acted oh so surprised when a car hit it a glancing blow, scaring the driver and sending sparks this way and that. There was the last time I tried to make my mark in the daylight hours. Later everyone awoke to find everything in the house was made of chocolate. I expected them to be grateful – even flattered. And Eddie pretended to be, but started sobbing suddenly. I'd been too much involved in my own thoughts to realise this kind of enterprise was unwanted. Put everything away and told them it was all right they could come on out. But just then the police arrived and I was blamed all over again.

Speaking of which – and here's a tale worth the telling – Empty Fred knows his way round a police disguise. But he gives himself away soon enough when he starts the talk – starts laughing and moving his arms quickly in a sort of chopping motion. His arms are too fast for folk around here – backs up his arguments with them and creates headaches from scratch. Wrong to make too much of an argument, people told him at first. Drift into sloth and go peaceably on your way. Fred took it badly – roofed a farmer with his car. Braked in time to greet the fella's wife a ways along.

Had a meeting in the bar about it when the mess had been flushed.

'The smoke and dust obscured even his gun that time.'

'I saw.'

'But the kill was prim.'

'Right – and long bloody overdue.'

'Tell me about it.'

Then it was off to the shrink to whom I'd been referred by the authorities. No sense elaborating but it all stemmed from an incident involving dogs and intense affection, you know the song. On this visit I only stared in through his window until he jerked the curtains closed – my first and last proper session the previous week had verged on the fatal for both of us. He sat there harping on about how a man like me should just take it easy and say whatever came into my head. Didn't believe me when I said that was my life in a nutshell.

'Would you like to talk about it?' he asked.

'If it'll get me off the hook with those bastards at the unit,' I said, 'I'd eat my own brittle grandmother.'

What I told the shrink

We'll skip the childhood bollocks and cut to the mayhem eh? England's a shower curtain for the modest butcher, as you know. Minotaur's always saying so long as you evade the spotlight you can learn all you want. 'Too much bleating and the true spice becomes a bright stew of obsolete crossways,' he reckons – so in the Shop o' Fury he hammers tears into coins and spoons strange, articulated soup all the time. 'Prayer loves detail – slows you down.'

'And delays the disappointment?' I offered once, but he just stared at me – face like a scone, you know. There he was, like, surrounded by radiator soil and little self-assembly resentment generators, accusing *me*.

But I didn't have anything better to do so I watched him prepare an ache channel in the sick air. 'Later I soak the bone in the dark,' he said, 'failing in rain and silently wheeling my hand, like so – that's to attract the inhabitants.'

'In – inhabitants?'

'Of fiendhouse – there's one in here.' And he held up the bone like a telescope to my eye – I saw rich illness and screaming smoke, yellow minds withdrawing and infinite.

'A crumb is logical, though discarded. Life is life.'

In the dark room ruins entire rushed up the walls, a distance quivering in old windows – then he slammed the bone down like an inverted glass, cutting off the process.

'Pour ill fate in their face and sew the wound alive.'

I'd heard of this before as Empty Fred had used a similar principle to etherically cut-and-paste a sort of horse stable on to some wasteland near his gaff. It was meant as a place for Godber's Troops to hide when the cops were after them. Empty Fred had joined the Troops because they were the only bastards distracted enough to ignore him. The downside was at regular intervals he'd be hauled out of bed and propelled through a hull door with only a parachute between him and the slamming palm of God. Reluctantly wore the uniform sometimes, blank epaulets staple-gunned to his shoulders – inverted commas I suppose, raised eyebrows, irony. That's how he meant it but they looked like banana peel to me, or the aura stain of his imminent death.

'What did you see in the betsy stick brother?' he asked, drinking.

'Scalped abdomen, hypodermic chaos, brains aborted, rope darkness, charring avatars. Mechanical canyon lined with waitresses. Anything pales after that brother. Stay away.'

And he planted oh so subtly the notion to boost the bone. 'Boost the bone,' he said. 'We'll be rich. Lobster lunches with the dead etc.'

But when the time came he was off on some practice drop into New Cross – bloody nightmare apparently. Parachutes everywhere, troops sobbing, screech of cars, twenty people dead.

Anyway so I got Eddie into the scam. Him, me and the

Rubitron went into town to test the wares in a cinema showing a director's balls-up of something that had been fine to begin with. No need for remorse if things went to hell.

'What did you see in the betsy stick brother?' Eddie asked, drinking.

'Only beauty,' I said.

'That's nuthin',' he laughed as we neared the venue. 'I once pressed the cheek of a cat and it let out a sort of laugh, like a chuckle or something.'

'Or something? Don't you know?'

'I sort of can't say if it was exactly—'

'Was it a *snigger* then?'

'Look it was a chuckle okay.'

'You getting all this Rube?'

'Every word.'

'You aren't a cop right Miss Ruby?'

'What's it to you? And anyway I'm not interested in.' And she fixed me with a stare and said:

'Little boys' games.'

Then she strutted off till the magnetic pull to follow her diminished.

'Suspect convenience re the knife Eddie.'

' "I had it because I love it." '

'That's your get-out eh? An invertebrate compensates for his lack with a sudden lunge. You'll fry.'

'Seated?'

'I imagine so.'

'So long as I'm seated.'

'It's curious how different fools are when completely toasted.'

'Different how?'

'More character. Variegation.'

'And corrugation?'

'You've got the idea. Darkness to show there's something unrevealed – like that dog over there. Keeps its mouth closed. So when it springs at you for no reason, gob railed with teeth, you know it all at once through the sudden contrast.'

'You mean it's holding something back.'

'For greater impact at the fine hour, that's right Sonny Jim.'

'If a dog explodes, do you call that ethnic?'

'What's the cause?'

'Prayer.'

'Yeah I think so.'

'What if the person praying didn't believe?'

'Then it was truly a miracle.'

Inside we dunked the frightener in a juice bucket, planted it near the speakers and waited for a reborn breeze to bless the cobwebs. Almost immediately spinelight circled the room and there swooped the downside. Abscess puppets resplendent in trailing gore, each skull as individual as a snowflake. A massive igneous brain dragging wires dumped itself on the front row. The air segmented, squirting blur-trains of spooky muscle toward us, which landed as crone-throated corpses in our laps. Dimmer ones were prowling up the aisle, I could see. The stench of fear and poached blood. Swooping shreds shrieked over our heads.

'Rude aren't they?'

But parts were already redissolving to leave only some hardening connective tissue on the walls.

Sniggering on the way out we were brought up sharp by the bloke on the door. There he was, punctate gill flanges and all. 'Bones is nuthin',' Eddie squawked but I shut him up – I could deal with this.

Tried a sort of punching gambit, with shouts and a murderous expression. Stood up to think it over again. Eddie dabbed gore from his muzzle and tried to see.

Reasoned with the bloke man-to-man. 'So there's corpses at large,' I began matter-of-factly. 'You'll have a paper face and eyelids like the wings of a moth before you really understand what happened just now. And so what? Spectres echo here anyway don't they?'

The doorman clutched his speech in bared teeth. 'Gorillas!' he said, and immediately said it again louder. He was the sort. Boot you in the gob and bye-bye accent. Luckily just then a few strays whistled out of a vent and tore off part of his forehead. Who had the whip hand on these mothers? Not me. Gave me the heebie-jeebies. Cosmic sepsis, ghost-stream, jellyheads – well that's all right if you can stand the pace. Everyone reckons spirits are a right laugh to flurry and snort over the houses – don't you believe it.

'So you used the core stick eh?' Bob rumbled later, glaring. 'There you go again agog at the wrong marvels. Know what I'd have done at your age if a being like Minotaur showed me the way?'

'Carve your initials on his face? Ha ha ha.'

Bob's eyes rolled up into his mind.

Of course we stay friends despite all this – just the other day me and the others were in the bar talking about Carver I think it was. 'The point is,' I said, 'a wrinkled brain like his is a geological mystery, rubber and passive.'

'For your sake,' Minotaur remarked, 'I hope it's that and nothing more.'

'And just what the hell do you mean by—'

—and Bob slammed in through the flap-dramatic door. 'I wish it was autumn, your race weeping by night, embraces up its sleeve and a knife in its hand. Goats stop talking, goats stop talking.'

'You all right Bob?'

'Do I look all right?'

'A drink for my friend Bob here – and one for yourself, we're all friends here aren't we?'

'For a week we are. Then . . .'

'Then?'

'Then spiders flex in the dark.'

'In the dark eh,' I said, nodding intensely. 'Spiders. Well now it's all becoming clear to me. Isn't it Eddie? Becoming clear.'

'Oh yes, clear all right.'

'Well that shows how much you know Eddie. It's as clear as my arse that's what. As clear as my arse my arse my stupid arse, that's what we know here though none of us has the balls to admit it. Bob here, this man here, he's as barking mad as anyone I've looked at in my life. He's almost extinct's what I think, and I for one—'

'Yes?' said Minotaur.

'You think I'll be held back now? I was about to say, yes, I for one am getting just the hell out of here before we're all of us, yes everyone, sucked into this bastard's game. Out of my way.'

'You'll pay for this.'

'Will I. We'll understand later who'll pay, Sonny Jim.'

So there I was in front of the firing squad and they asked me as they do about the last notion – have you any final notions? they asked as they were strapping on the old blindfold.

'Yes,' I said, 'I'd like to tell you about the time I rode on a dog and thought for a moment I was a better man than I am.'

'Well don't keep us poised here all afternoon,' they said, 'it's not healthy for any of us.'

What I told the firing squad

I was incredibly horny when I was a young 'un – smoke the colour of biscuit came out of my nose when I saw the curvature on a woman. I was calm only when knocked oblivious by a restaurant swingdoor and how often does that really happen.

Give me moans in bloom any day. Ruby Thunderhead tied her hair back so hard her face split down the middle. Backbone glistened and grew. Bubbling forehead of transformation. There's a real woman for you. Told her she looked like an explosion and she responded by becoming exactly that. Met her in a mutant salon. Tubes and ducts were shoving out of her face to beat the band. You could do that for a living I said.

'Earn an audience with nineteen valves coming out of my face? What kind of audience?'

'The forgiving kind.'

Blinked and she was still there. Morality like a diving board and an arse the angels born in heaven would kill for. Clothing was discarded like pinpulled grenades – frantic isn't the word.

That was the start. My cool demeanour comes of being

used for target practice as a child – all that ducking, wincing and screaming, I got it out of me early.

'So what d'you do?'

'I'm serenaded by bullshit.'

'For a living?'

'I seek solace in revenge and suspicion. Implode and waste everyone's sweet time.'

'And Eddie?'

'That bastard? Know why he's so strange? His ears are older than the rest of him. His ears are seventy-eight years old.'

'Why should that cause such a problem?'

'He's known it since he was three. Think of it.'

'I'm thinking.'

'Well? Three. And so does everyone else know. About the ears I mean, the age. It's how he's identified. It's on all the police records. Become the way the bastard identifies himself.'

'There's worse ways.'

'Like what?'

'Beliefs?'

'You must be joking.'

'Courage?'

'Not bloody likely.'

'Betting strategy?'

'You having me on? If he sees a nag with the right number of legs he stuffs dosh in its mouth. Doesn't know there's a better way.'

'Is there?'

'A sea monster surely,' said Eddie when I told him about her.

'No,' I assured him. 'The corpsed soil is always under her, with shameful direct sunlight.'

'She'll deflate your stern with a needle brother.'

He was surprised as my real fetish at the time was tying up snort-laughing barmaids with bundles of my own nerves – a restraint the thickness of cotton so naturally their struggle was all pretend. Meanwhile I'd tog up as a camel and set fire to my arse. I was surprised to discover years later that this was considered normal. Apparently if there weren't at least a dozen silver-painted midgets and a chariot involved the experiment was a non-starter round there.

Eddie told me I should get rid of her by any means available but I was balmy and charmed. 'You'll have no physical pain Eddie, not at first. Life measured in tides of snot, whispered like memorial curses. Movement by the tiny privilege stepladder. Dark afflicted years of assignment to the business corridor, then the last.'

'Explain.'

'Age Eddie. Veins under onion paper. Bed for a statue and a dead man's hairstyle.'

'No.'

'Oh, yes. Pitifully aproned and weeping, there's your end.'

'I'm not replying till you change what you just said.'

'I mean no harm.'

'Just don't try it all right?'

'Bob's got so much metal in his face there's a danger of changing the magnetic polarities of the planet Eddie.'

'Bob has no metal in his face.'

'Well he might.'

'Stick to the facts brother or don't say anything.'

'You've had quite enough, is that the song? I've gone just a little too far this time. Pushed the boundaries further than you ever dreamed possible and now you're afraid –

afraid of your own complicity in the matter and intent on kicking my blameless arse from here to eternity for the crime of expressing myself in terms normally reserved for saints and waiters.'

Eddie merely gulped at his pint and avoided my eye.

'So there's the final argument of those who never had enough tit in their early years – bitterness at those who have overcome the trauma in their own unique and personal way.'

'That's it,' he said, and stood like a decided man. Two hours later he was in the same position and other drinkers had come and gone, time called and the doors closed – activity surrounded the statue of this once angry man. A doctor was summoned who tapped him with tiny hammers – turned out the outermost layer of the fool had turned to flint. 'He's in there, living in his usual way,' said the doc, packing his gear, 'but none of it's visible to the eye. Feed him plenty of straw and talk to him about the league tables. He'll soon see his immobile state has no consequence in the world, same as when he's up and about like a good 'un.'

'Thanks doc,' I said, and opened space to visit Minotaur, whose opinions scared me less these days. Voodoo air and autopsy humour. Minotaur wept minnows and laughed poison gas. That's how much of an impression he made on me and frightened the others when he claimed to know demons and to halve his salary with the devil himself. 'Killjoys' he called those who ran. Had a style pedal attached to his arm so he could punch you in the manner of various celebrities. Mother Theresa would deliver a haymaker to the belly and Nixon would slap.

His abode steamed with abominations.

'Elastic bats eh?'

He poured a drink. 'Goat water brother. Drink it and your skin will become lace, tearing with dust.'

'One man's poison,' I said, accepting the glass. 'Now what's Eddie up to really d'you think, in himself?'

'Neglecting his studies like a man possessed. And more which I am unable to describe in your simple language.'

'Am I supposed to be frightened?'

'Respectful brother – of Satan.'

'Not Satan again – give it a rest brother.'

'Satan never rests.'

'No wonder he's so uptight. Sling me the paper.'

'At a time like this brother. You'll learn the hard way.'

'Yeah the hard way, whatever you say brother – sling it over, there's a thing in there about lard and creation.'

'There is nothing in there about lard and creation.'

'I'm saying there is brother – give it here.'

But every single story in the rag was about Bob – and every one stated that he had been seen strangling a swan and then tearing off its bill to use as a mouthpiece on a black, antique telephone. 'The type you'd see in an old, cruel film,' went the story. This event occurred at some big social function and Bob had been there in smart clobber – probably with the express purpose of assaulting the animal. More than forty people saw the attack and each told a variation of the same savage yarn. And so another day's paper was filled.

The main editorial went on about 'servitude' and 'clemency', concluding that everything was 'washed up' for the poor wretch.

'The press are always the last to catch on aren't they?' I remarked to Minotaur, but he eyed me with doom-heavy disapproval.

I persisted. 'Headlocked morons I mean. Still reading cloth books probably. About ducks and so on.'

'Through compromise we travel, through social graces we skid.'

Minotaur spoke of universal gifts. For the grand embryonic wrong, grief. For the operating nerve of God, resentment. For me, exhaustion.

'The skeleton in the egg eh?'

'If you like.'

'If I like – that's a good one. You never stop do you brother?'

And now I recall the days when just this sort of exchange would make me burst out to the glee of the gutter press – BASTARD MAKES FREE WITH METAL PIPE AND DOESN'T HELP US PRETEND WE DON'T KNOW WHY – that sort of thing.

Bloody murder was still popular then and had everyone guessing, or able at least to frown. Have another was the cry. Have a double. Then the outrage.

So anyway after discussing Bob and Eddie a while and consulting the Horned One on various matters I left Minotaur and joined Ruby in a primeval swamp, which is what we did for fun at this point in our disastrous relationship. We walked out into evolution and faced one another, the mud-infested drool continuum swarming around us. 'I can't believe it began here,' she began to say but I shut her up. Bats and slow-worms started sniggering. 'Where's Bob then?' she asked.

'In a dungeon enquiring whether they really suppose he's guilty.'

'White with mishap.'

'What do you think.'

'What's the charge?'

'Walking on the ceilings of their gravity.'
'What exactly did he do?'
'You really want to know?'

What I told Ruby Thunderhead

Moscow I suppose was where it really began. Veal was the most important thing in that town. Basements were full of it – those that weren't full of my nose-steam and the entrails of bears I'd brought there under false pretences and dispatched with a jerryhammer – Arthur and Peter and the gas meter smiled at my entry, dragging these spoils and others which are still too recent to mention without risk of arrest. Place me where you will in the cannon but don't fire till I'm done.

Three times I provided veal for the community, and each time I had no memory of the event. Bakers and lechers winked and made remarks – but it was only later, when I left and received letters from a sweetheart with photographs and accusations, that I knew or believed that I had killed anything more substantial than a few tiresome waiters. Veal, it seemed, was a delicacy, and I'd bring it into the tavern on the corner, my coat exploding with crusted snow as I hauled the carcass on to the bar. 'There's your demon,' I said, 'and the antlers are the so-called horns. So don't let me hear your superstitious nonsense till you see a real one.'

Serve me right, of course, they did see a real one – the very next day. Bellowing and ramming children in the nursery. Teachers in tears and folk in the police station with rakes and rifles and a tracking dog for shouting through the woods and hunting the terror down. The only thing I knew about demons was what I'd read, and I was filled with a fear that gripped me, lifted me into a car, and drove me two thousand miles in the opposite direction to a stranger's house, where I related the hunt in perfect detail. I've always been marginal, me.

Oilskin-clad artists walked down the three short steps to my next local and broke wind at each step, so that everyone began punching them and reciting the rules. They said it was victimisation and everyone told them it was like hell. It was exactly. Grand old masters burnt their own works and scratched their beards with both hands until the blood flowed. Ghosts pretended to be window glass and eavesdropped on our every conversation. The wise bailed out, cursing those they left behind. It usually ended with something like 'and I hate you all'. There were times when I believed this was the only way to address a member of the artistic community. Later I sold a spicy doughball in the street for eighty quid because the fool thought I was someone else. There was my first lesson in how to progress in this world.

And when entering a new neighbourhood I was careful to take with me my face and, hung behind it, my opinions. These concerned an apple-size brain lost in paradise, nerve surveillance, comic united money, morality guarantees, applause outworn, herbicides stroking the garden, blood-covered definitions, mechanical whirring fossils, batwing prams, poverty and drear shade, crow blossom and infant chains. Catch elves and weep – woe to worms in disguise.

Nobody was coerced into frightening me regularly as I tried to settle in – people seemed to do it of their own volition, testifying in detail as to their very specific reasons. I hate you because . . . and the rest would be so personal and idiosyncratic I would weep at the diversity of mankind. Hate, I told them, is a poor fruit for such a rich branch.

These taunts were worth all the fun I'd had in the past – these jabs of knives the spice I'd brazened my life for seeking.

As a token of my esteem I gave a stare of malicious intent to everyone in the town.

Eking out a living from beetroot and eyeshadow in the darkest alleys I could find, I told people I was a leper and that was good enough for them. I heard every variety of shriek in the first year, every kind of laughter in the second. Scorn and abasement go hand in hand when a nation comes to rest in its own guilt. Gnashing at the bit they were, to run off and tell no one. Nick their evasions and in five minutes they're barking like dogs and secreting gob-foam to beat the band.

Little did I know Bob was a few miles under the sink, a castaway with a squirming beard. That was the manner of his home back then. Dangles of nerves betrayed the subway roofs to a sensitivity no one suspected. An entire ganglion system tangled the roots and shrieked with pain amid the screaming trainbrakes. There's the true living city for you. Trickles whisper in abattoir drains and all's well with the world.

Score and number were loosed in a spray of phlegm as Bob counted his arrests. 'A thousand reasons more and conspiracies are no longer necessary,' he said the first time I met him, and he viewed the galore of allegations with pride. Sat there relating a plan to starve the destroyer by lack of targets. 'Notice the ears on either side of that apple? Now tell me the world's not collapsing.'

'So how'd you come to be here brother?'

'Educated in a cave by the white daughter of cannibalism, bled and saved by a doubting priesthood, I ran like buggery as soon as I saw an opening – flood and firestorm couldn't stop me as I undertook that journey – went to Eddie's crypt. There were rows of heads and concealed traps along the quiet aisle. Under no circumstances was I going to ask his help, just hide there till the storm had blown over – or Eddie caught me and I had to punch out to show what a mistake I'd made. Some roaring sound at the back of the chamber but I ignored it. What a fool I was. That day was the last me and my priest would spend apart.'

'Didn't mix then?'

'My brain and teeth struggled to fit, caked with textbooks. Deafening blast as I said hello. Shocks ran up my arm as I tried to salute. We are bones in disguise.'

'Tell me about this Eddie.'

'Bastard. Wore gym shorts to a funeral. Berated him later and he said, "Yes I wore shorts – that's why I understood the jeering." Useful bloody lot he is as a pallbearer or whatever he calls himself.'

'Is that how he sees himself then?'

'As a bastard? Certainly. And nobody has done it better. With a blank face the bastard froze everyone by leaving the fridge open and wielding a fan – speculation was no longer needed in determining the depth of his evil.'

'Well now, what shall we do with you?'

'Stab me if you can enjoy it – but not if it feels like a duty. Stab me vertically if I'm lying down and horizontally if I'm running.'

And so I was introduced to one and all. Fred was a simple man but a complex woman. 'I take it you're armed?'

'I *beg* your pardon?'

'You heard. And are going to tell me no. Your kind make me sick.'

And he walked away with one fist out in front of him like a Dalek. There's a strange one, I thought.

'And here's Eddie – he'd be using his halo for a cock ring if he was broad enough.'

'Pleased to meet you Eddie,' I said. There was a piece of brain coral on the table. 'What's this when it's at home?'

'A mandate to destroy.'

'Well . . . then.'

And within weeks we were best of friends.

'By your ocean-floor standards we're all of us heroes Eddie. From baptism font to wrist-bloodied basin eh? If I were you I'd be climbing my own face for worry.'

'Now explain that statement.'

'Your fate Eddie. Jostled in a plain van and all sharps confiscated. Look at him lads. Eddie was unmoored from coherence in his early years – weren't you Eddie?'

'You bastard I'll kill you.'

'Dent my stovepipe neck will you.'

'Yes.'

'Have me digesting my teeth.'

'Yes.'

'You'll need more help than you'll get.'

And he flung himself at me with all the wit he could muster. At the time I couldn't have told you what he wanted to achieve, but with the wisdom of years I see he was trying to do me harm. It was in his yelling bloody murder and punching the front of my face. There was even gore – a sure sign something's amiss. His reflection in the pub mirrors moved at exactly the same rate he did. That's the clincher for me, in looking back on it. He was an angry man, and more than that I could say if I knew it.

Bob had a habit of articulating what was on everyone's minds. He knew I hated clowns and gave me a rifle. There was no doubt as to his meaning. He was always doing that sort of thing. Then when he met old Minotaur at the Shop o' Fury he returned with the tale – something about a demon. 'And seaweed made of elastic,' he snorted.

'My nerves wouldn't stand it,' said Fred.

'*Your* nerves?' Bob shouted. 'You weren't there, tomb addict. The bumps of my spine scraping in its jaws . . .' he remembered, shuddering.

'My nerves wouldn't stand it,' said Fred.

'Have you been listening to me?' bellowed Bob, grabbing Fred's ear and making another loud noise which contained no words. This was done for the purpose of making Fred jump or react, though he appeared to be falling asleep like the bastard he was. 'Need these bones and you're defeated.'

'Hello,' sneered Fred, 'he's off again.'

'I mean it. You'll pay for your nonchalance – when randomness lashes your dream.'

'Oh it'll lash my dream will it – just like that? Scenic disaster and just deserts-a-go-go. As you look on unsurprised.'

'Correct.'

'With one nose facing west and the other dripping like a main.'

Bob stayed stock still, a riot of responses clashing behind his stony face.

'So why don't the limp silhouettes of entering phonies trip and fall if there's a god and justice?'

'You ask too many questions comrade.'

'Yes Fred,' I said, 'why d'you rush in without thinking?'

'I'm being timed.'

Good answer, I thought, despite myself.

At the gallery Eddie catalogued his experiences. Failure, ice cracking, violence, a colourless tomorrow. A fresh outpouring of tears greeted the recollection.

'It permeated your nasal passages I suppose,' I said, not really listening. 'Listen, are these paintings really necessary? Maybe a monocle would make the monkey look more graceful.' A massive migration of ideas occurred from my gob to Eddie's brain, where they instantly died.

'What do you mean?' he said.

Argument. Shouting. Punched him and he rolled up with bulging, ghoulish eyes. True colours.

I still couldn't understand the scam. Look at the picture over there of a gilly fiend – who'd pay for that? Walked up to get a closer look at the thing without realising I was approaching the reflection of the painting in a huge mirror – by the time I was stood an inch from the fiend I'd passed through the mirror and blown the whole thing.

Well you've guessed the rest – alternate reality, the fiend was real, the devil himself, cellars of wrenched hungmen, glass hands of steam and thought, a havoc angel tending his creep in a scabby cavern. The devil was no more than a tense, contentious lattice, at the front of which, like a bride fronting a wedding train, was a monster like a fish on its haunches, picking martyrdom thorns out of his teeth. 'Your hopes?' he asked.

'Groundless.'

'So far so good then, after a fashion. But which fashion, I wonder. Creeping despair?'

'Yes.'

'I see. Mooning toward the end of a life which is, in all senses, a waste of time.'

'Nail on the head, sunshine.'

'And loving it I suppose.'

'Of course. I'm not one to gash my wrist in an ice cave and carve my features in the frozen garnet. You know better than that I hope.'

'Learn what you know and forget what I told you,' said the demon, 'polarities are for the birds. But one is left to wonder how long you've been this way.'

'What way?'

'Barking,' he said.

'Long enough,' I said, 'to know its value.'

'How long, I asked, have you been in this condition?'

'How far can a stain grow before it can no longer truly be called a stain?'

But the answer was, of course, from the very beginning. I was pushed into the world wrinkled as a walnut – couldn't they see I wasn't prepared? Sputed into the dirt of this century. Monosodium glutamate and cynical laughter. And there didn't seem to be any doubt I'd be dead again later, bones picked sky white. Doomed as a jubilee hog. A bonemaker.

Couldn't believe what I was expected to do. Breathe constantly. Talk to those who addressed me, merely because they addressed me. This was life? What could I do with these legs and this face except kick and curse those I encountered?

The devil heard the thought and his eyes rolled up like

punters' at a carnival. 'Really – "I didn't ask to be born." A new skull's routine argument.'

'You'll believe me when I'm finished – and more.'

'Much more?'

'Well it'll have to be won't it?'

'Tell it then – and make it charming.'

'Charming? Oh well then – here's how it all began.'

What I told the devil

Red memories thick with ambulances. My father. Through his beard came a century's worth of wisdom and not one coherent word. But he conveyed by some means that a man should stand still and take everything he was dealt. I hit him so hard he forgot his own name and the nature of our relationship, at which I found myself penniless and stark in a town they don't even talk about on maps. Salty streets, cobbled faces, ladles in the drains, beaks in the gutter, chefs with whips and the pig-ignorant peering down chimneys. I told them they were on the wrong track, they sneered and pelted me with tar and thatch, fat and kelp, lard and marge, absolution and pity, and a kind of religious feeling of cleansing and purification I hadn't felt since I was an infant. Sacks of stale charm were left in doorways and everyone knew what it meant for those inside – brats gathered it up before the postman could shoot a single round, delivering the bales to old women in the keelhaul quarter, who would eat it slowly, chomping and never getting any bigger. This sort of blear enterprise was considered jib bollox in that conurbation.

Flammables were treated the same way, except that

dough was placed in the eyesockets of those who left them and later retrieved and fired in an oven, at which everyone would gather to warm themselves. The flammables themselves went into the river with all the other trash.

My first lesson in the matter of death was when a man below my window in Felt Street shouted out and I ran to look – there he was strangling a hen, and as I looked closely I saw that it was only because the hen bore the man's facial features. I shouted out, 'So what if it's identical?' and he was so surprised that he ran – but took the hen with him.

I realise now, years later, that the hen was in fact a mere extension of the man's body, and the man, knowing for the first time the full horror of this, was wrestling against all likelihood to rid himself of the protuberance.

But back then I reacted like the callow youth I was. There was no order to my thought or face as I entered the barracks and mounted a guard dog, exciting the troops and provoking bets and insult. I heard one man add the term 'Holy Man' to the front of my name – or thought I did. Which was the last thing I needed in m'darkness, I can tell you.

Sometimes in those early days there was a fair full of sleepwalking clowns and beard-eating men and fiery women flirting with the dogs and punching the workers. One of the clowns stole a horse and had to be shot twice before he'd slow down.

And there was a giant which the children set alight. When the giant burnt it left a helterskelter skeleton with fleshrind and eyes here and there – and it was surprising how soon everyone lost interest. Flames were the rage round there as I've said and once that was done I think everyone wanted to drink or kill. Flirting with danger, they called it.

Slippery dogs left the scene with the guilt we human beings were no longer able to feel.

In the square, caged monks yelled at the top of their voices till they were sure they were alone, then fell to gambling. Someone had to do something practical round here. But I wouldn't keep away. It was from these monks that I learnt about my earliest ancestor, Gibby. Axing the tabulations of a medieval scientist was the one thing he was remembered for – that and his attempts to charm the birds out of the trees with a bow and arrow. 'I'll make them respect me if the Lord allows,' he said loud enough for the Mayor to shout an opinion which contradicted the trend of these actions. My ancestor was so proud he hid his face against the taut string of the bow, letting fly an arrow at the Mayor's good heart. Everything – and I mean everything – fell to pieces for his family in the dark days which followed. Bargains were struck in the dank hallways outside Gibby's cell until he was informed he'd be strung on a branch and made to stay there.

'The tree hasn't been sprouted that could hold me,' he laughed, breathing heavily through his mouth, and died the next day trying to kick the spectators from a lofty height.

Killings were not uncommon in that age – rather more common than today in fact. Proven crimes were less frequent because aliens tended to fry the meat and dispose of it through their gill arches. Digging for bones would create nothing but great heaps of earth and red-faced, angry diggers with spades and near-broken spirits. Nothing worse than a man who's dug all day and found his own reflection in a shallow pond.

So anyway having got the information from the monks I was about to leave but one of 'em grabbed me arm, thrusting his boiled face through the bars. 'Sin and elements, abyss weather, serpents of human blood, drugs of the great master, timed generation, the burden of chickens, in the morning everything a cop hates wakes and takes the crowd, not a crime was committed to calm the frenzy of the imagination. Not until you, that is. And how did you do it? Eluded a barrage of facts, propagated tourists, ballooned the map, moved the horizon like a chain-link fence, your head tight as the inside of a baseball, neighbourhood eaten alive. And those who understood not, they said: stone the advantage, demand nothing, appear simple, explore defeat and roar public compliments. Vanity is leafless 'neath its own garden, background stars fastened like flystuds. But we know the truth eh boy? Have frogs home and flick jello snot at your mother. Wound General Grant hard in the front, just for starters. Your spine needn't be compromised – soon you'll belong in permanent collision. Promise me boy, you'll leave this place with a better plan than you joined it.'

It was a nasty shock extended for years in every direction. Forgot about it till a moment ago.

Ventured back the next day. Morphine morning like a cloak, you know. But the gamblers weren't there. Brushstroke dollar and mechanical fountain. Desert popcans, crusted. Evidence of past fun, a skull abandoned on a trampoline.

And I thought – parts become outdated, it's a hood with smile, it's sleeves on cars, it's the norm, who can keep up?

The snow landed all at once to save time.

Bleating mavericks crowded me as I tried to move down the narrow streets. I kicked through the scales which avalanched from their eyes. I didn't need this distortion to contend with and I started to stumble, the embattled rind of my good nature crisping like bacon. Fever dreams. Towering kebabs drippled with sachet sauce. Mystery holes in the skyroof. Bugs in combat, eyestalks clashing. Leonine roars from children. A swarming heaven of cackhanded guardians. Head splitting like a pomegranate.

Kept hearing about a whore who read fortunes on the side. Spooky rumours. Born by means of a bonesaw. Basement of abominations. No saliva. Decided to seek her out.

Held a tiny jade effigy of Lee Oswald in the pouch of each cheek. That's how serious I was. And she didn't disappoint. Consulted hourly a wisp-haired shrunken head on a fob chain. Dynamited fish like she invented the game. Nose made of cement. Nothing wrong with that except it never dried and people would push it into a shape of their choice as though it were putty. The room was filigreed with stress vents, prayer code, flesh phones, barter bones, fungal earlobes and acupuncture stakes.

'First things first,' she said. 'Speak any languages?'

'Darkness,' I said.

'One language.'

'And depravity, a little – enough to get by.'

'Enough depravity to get by,' she muttered, writing. 'Right. Now take this dagger, close your eyes, and touch your nose.'

'With the dagger?'

'That's right. Good, very good. Here's a tissue. Have you ever eaten a tapir?'

'Tapirs no . . .'

'Because they're really good.'

'Right.'

'So what have you been doing with yourself? Walking heavy with alcohol and conjuring antagonists out of empty air, no doubt.'

'How d'you know?'

'I know all. I've got a blasted pyrex replica of your arse under a bell jar in the other room.'

'Beg pardon?'

'Pride of place. Next to the shredder.'

'Ay?'

'Let's get down to business, corky. How much d'you know about the world?'

'I'm guessing the gods are big, their cups an' tea things also.'

'Well that's as good a place to start as any. When I was a kid you couldn't keep me away from gore. But people mature. Gas grows their hands and they gain confidence. Bangles bow me and dry my time – I'm like a tree knuckling defiance against the rain. Consoled by a mantel trophy of husked ambition. Do you know what I still now plan to achieve?'

I shook my head.

'Everything here will become edible – because I'll make it so. I'll need nothing more expert than a trowel, a flirting badger, ten skills I don't possess, a fable recited from memory, a kennel the size of an aircraft hangar and a bagel which speaks. Nouns will be its only problem, for reasons you will understand when that is all you've left to understand.'

'Why, though?'

'Food on this planet doesn't speak unless spoken to – by which time it's too late. Does that seem fair to you? And I say it's not. Guilt freezes the mistake, perfect preservation for fifty years or more. See for yourself.' And she opened a bladder fridge to display its moth lining and closed vents. She went on a while about life being the second-by-second process of strenuously resisting annihilation, while at the same time remaining flexible. 'The whole world's a high wall of escape, a backdown taunt for the bottle-brave. I loved atoms just enough to inhabit them – perhaps too much. They were aspects I felt I had to deal with. But you'll find most citizens slam their faculties and amplify alarm. Families smile in debt, calamities on account to keep things shallow, believing the siphon of understanding'll dry by their determination. In books there's nothing of the fish covered in the coldness of the sea, or the feeling of a star touching space. Bad for business.'

'Is it now.'

'Doesn't feed the disease.'

'Surely it can. Air's pushed from pages as they close, shelves of suffocation die aching.'

'Not the same thing boy. Put on a cape and tell 'em you're here – see the reaction you get.'

'I'll get a reaction.'

'I know you will.'

Expect bastards and you'll get them, she said. Clever bird – never explained what would happen if I didn't and I soon found out.

And there's where I found my way. Opened morning's curtains to see a world covered by a sheet of society.

Trouble's the only thing which can result from posing in a doorway with your trousers on only one leg. And it's the bare leg, not the trousered one, which will be the cause of that trouble. Arm yourself with a knife my friend, and beware the police.

Trouble with the devil

The devil gazed into the dregs of his pint and puckered his lips thoughtfully. 'And that's really all you have to say in your defence.'

'That and the fact that my manhood belongs in a whaling museum.'

'Yes, well I'd like to say you've deceived no one and they're bereft. But all are lied to and satisfied.'

'Low expectations you mean.'

'And crap judgement.'

'You disapprove then?'

'Oh no – the sword of truth's rusted in its scabbard and I'm delighted. But today's trespass is the first of many.'

'I'm not sure I follow the gallopede of shite you call an argument.'

'You're due to abuse the flux glass again in future and for this I'm due to punish you now.'

'And how will you apply this so-called punishment? Belt me with a hoof I suppose.'

'No, we have core creatures here for that sort of business.' And he gestured to something like a lobster drinking catlike from a kidney dish. Roach the size and shine of a patent leather shoe.

'Oh I didn't see it before. So am I really to pay for something I haven't done yet?'

'Past, present, future – all is one.'

'In what sense?'

'In the sense that at all times you are a bastard.'

'Ah now I differ there – I recall an occasion I was a world-class hero and lovely boy. It began in the metallic reign of hypocrisy, all gaudy and bejewelled with tumbling midgets. Advantages in operation, Eddie ventured into the traffic . . .' And here I told a tale so full of wonder and magic I nearly blinded myself. Whole empires were rendered in fly-leg detail, mangrove domes sweating rain, enchantments nabbed amid the closed snores of the innocent, balloon-trousered princes punching like a girl, convict voyages to temperatures unknown, expensive wounds inflicted by nutters, dogs wearing lipstick, litter temples and sacrifice. Hours had passed and I was just getting into the swing. 'So there I was, ringside in a scuba mask, a gimmick I thought would distract the victor from punching Eddie. "Stay down Eddie, stay down! Everyone's laughin' at ya!" Eddie looked up with an unseeing eye. His cauterised innocence was still smoking, as you can imagine. And—'

'Stop, stop, *stop* you bastard!' shouted the devil suddenly, and glared a while indignant. 'What the *bloody* hell are you playing at? Are you mad? D'you think I've no better way to spend m'time than listening to some stancing disaster recycle his snot for hours on end?'

'Not by the look of it, fishface.'

'What?'

'Well look at you sat there like a hollow chocolate Buddha, you're hardly busy.'

'What do you think these are for, you moron?' he demanded, twanging a lattice rope like a spider testing its web. 'The hub and spoke of evil, this is. I run it all from here. What do you do? You and your strutting arrogance. Yes, you. Whoring after your destiny with your multi-petalled psychosis all a-flutter.'

'Oh now it all comes out.'

'Yes it does actually, yes.'

'You're just an old codger aren't you? You're never punching me with that flipper of yours – tell me you're fooling.'

A force in the atmosphere swirled about him, sparking like darkness. Head muscles were breathing in the red jawpush of transformation, shoulders swelling, and his body balled up like a badger pelted with acorns, punching out steel spikes as thick as streetcones. A music-hall asteroid.

It sounds mean but I was totally bored by these eruptions. The only time this sort of thing happened to me it occurred in a way nobody ever believed when I talked about it. Of course the core creature scuttled toward me but I stamped on it same as I would a financial adviser, leaving a jagged mess with clusters of neckteeth broken and sputtery, so I was all right there.

Meanwhile though the old sharps were popping off John Satan like seeds off a pinecone and he said my worse nightmares were due to become a reality. I knew myself well enough to know what this would mean – pasta, golf, toffs, opera and dizzy birds talking shite, all somehow rolled into one. The fallen thorns were spores, dragonteeth germinating to beat the band. Mutants, truelove. Hollering and a-bellowing out of the earth – and I saw the combination of horrors I just described had made them empty, like paper lanterns. Even so they swiped flaming torches off the cavern walls and ran at me. Pursuit down tunnels, shrieks, freakish shadows, the whole nine yards.

As any athlete with a flexible gob will tell you, run focused and fast enough and you leave your ego behind, wobbling in the air like a mansize soap bubble. Caught a glimpse of mine just before the torches made contact and it was a magenta gas cell in the shape of a Ford Escort. Then it ignited, killing my tormentors as I burst through the mirror in an explosion of dry cornflakes and litterleaves. Eddie was still slumped in a corner and less than a minute had passed. But was it art?

Decided to lie low a while in another country – but returned starving for lack of cooperation. At the rail of the liner I wept at the sight of my homeland, sun shining through a wound in my shoulder. Surely a balanced life could be had here.

So I found a dark place but not too dark to transform myself into a pile of muscle and swallow the air which others needed to breathe well. In a corner I looked like a deck of plate fungus merely. This was the way a real man made a living in those days. Houses surrounded by trees could be almost covered by pulsating muscle flanges and appear normal to a dog in the sidecar of a passing motorcycle. And so these mysteries went unchallenged and unknown.

The vampires though, there's a tale. One that bothered me more than the others – a darting one with shapeless management ideas and undisclosed dreams who didn't know a window from a hole in the ground. Severed arteries with a bottle opener and chugalug. Hadn't the malevolence for it – took him on a haunting once and he stood singing with flowers in his hands – strange man with nothing but his ideas and consistency to keep him going. And he asked what the rest of us had. Faith, I said, in something better. I'll stay as I am, he said, as if he knew something we didn't.

Well anyway one afternoon we all appeared at the doorstep of Eddie's gallery and told him there were things inside we wanted to burn and throw. He asked if it was the paintings and we said yes that was it – of course he tried slamming the door but we were barrelling in all shouts and hilarity, tossing beer glasses and belching to beat the band. So this vampire I described before started winding an old monkeybox grind-organ and weeping like a trooper. Under dim light you understand. I flew at him in a rage but of course he vanished – looked up and saw him hung from a ceiling inverted. 'Well at least you're acting the part at last,' I told him, and at that he went limp, dropped everything including the monkeybox which hit me a glancing blow off the face and batted open, revealing to us the fact that its internal mechanism was nothing but bone, dry muscleweb and insect dust. 'No sense trying to make amends with this little display,' I said, resolved now that I'd got the full measure of the bastard. 'Eh lads? He's not to be trusted with beer or anything – and where's the bottle-opener you shite?'

The fiend didn't want to reply so there was nothing more to be had from him except visual information.

'We don't rely on you,' I said, and punched a portrait to show him. Of course the painting began to moan like a clubbed mime. I was so embarrassed I shouted the order to torch the place to cover the unearthly noise, and strung out the syllables like this. 'T-o-r-c-h-t-h-e-b-l-o-o-d-y-p-l-a-c-e!'

But everyone had gone home in utter boredom by then and only Eddie remained, standing there. Of course I looked at him with the kind of contrition I kept in a vault for such purposes. 'Look Eddie,' I said. 'I don't really want to burn this place of yours. These paintings are a blessed gift to mankind. Go forth and be merry.'

'You've stalked me for the last time,' he choked, shaking, and pulled a knife.

'Now there Eddie, go on that way and you'll find I die and you'll have blood everywhere in here. That's a real danger.'

And he was lunging at me with the shiv. That's the last time I remember Eddie doing anything really normal. After that he got to taking fish for walks and baking felt and blaming others for the shape of his heart. It's hard to be sanguine about such sharp misery. Wouldn't we all shoot a mayor or two for a few laugh-lines?

A week later Bob told me Eddie had folded the scam and sold everything in it to Minotaur. 'Why?' I asked.

'Because you and everyone else kept dragging vampires in there,' he gasped as if it were obvious.

Here's where Bob really started pushing the limit. Built a three-legged man out of marzipan, dubbed him 'Mr Trojan' and claimed to quote from the bastard: 'On gold comes their cold jest/with wine in flood upon his rage/and the heaviest hillside hid his questions.'

'You're asking for it brother.'

'Cicada mascot/airlock honeysuckle/a garden of roses/each with a pulse.'

'Cut it out brother.'

'The iron hand held the blade and went by choice to God/And God, nothing in his fire, returned every stroke save one – the wish for others' freedom.'

'Mr Trojan's looking ill,' I said, melting its face off with a lighter.

And it emitted a tiny scream.

Sleight of hand changed Bob into a man of honour. Burnished and proud. But it was only his reflection in a slick of lager and the lights swinging to bloom his shadow on the curved wall – you could see him thinking, yes I'm a braillefaced god, knowing it as true despite the lies he used to disguise it.

Liking harm and safety in equal measure, he punched a gran and ran home, forgetting his keys wallet passport incriminating photos and bottles of DNA for subsequent whole-body replication in a police lab – all this was found on the scene, where the gran was laughing with the honour of the meeting and clutching a hunk of his hair.

The police pinned up a Wanted poster of Bob's face and head, and every dog who saw it fell instantly in love with him. 'See,' I smirked, nudging him with both elbows at once, 'you're a pin-up, my son.'

'For dogs,' he clarified, enraged.

'It's a start.'

'Some are probably police dogs brother. Look at that one.' And he pointed to the face of an alsatian which had appeared at the window, panting steam.

Tried getting him used to dogs by belting him regularly with a fibreglass spaniel but he wouldn't have it – said there were more crucial things and showed me a hexagonal hole in space. Said we were in a hive reality and didn't know it. Ignored him till he hinted it was a fine way out of trouble.

Shortly after which he attacked a swan at this stuck-up affair and during his arrest some assistance including a full-nelson was provided. I suppose that about brings us up to date, darling.

Trouble with Ruby Thunderhead

The swamp receded in a crackling permafrost and we were sat indoors. I looked down to discover I was tied to a chair. Ruby was staring at me with concentration – but as she stood it was clear she'd long ceased contemplating the beauties of my yarn. Leaning down, she plucked a thick vein out of my arm and strode across the room trailing it over her shoulder like an extension lead to busy herself with its manipulation over a series of hooks and pulleys. The vein strung out like a reel but squealed like rubber, spraying a fine bloodcloud as I flinched and tried to explain.

'Watch it babe, er . . . Don't mind Bob now, I mean, he's all right – saw him doing a puzzle the other day and he was having a bit of trouble with it like and you shoulda seen him. Pounding on the puzzle, bleeding from the ears – he'll do us all proud one day. For instance. Town destroyed by swarm. You and I would detect mayhem and wild company. That scene is something he'd see technically, the bee the media the crowds. That's as far as it'd go.'

A string of flesh tautened, pushing a lamp from a table.

'That er – that reminds me of that time, ha ha. Swanned

into the bar pretending I was recently spurned in love and, gaining the sympathy of one and all, you see, drank enough on their pity to drop the act in a flood of gob saliva and eleven punches upside the face from Bob, while Eddie held my arms so far out of the way they broke at the shoulders. By God though it was a night to remember, that. What man doesn't remember his twentieth birthday? Wilder spit I never aimed, by God. Sweetheart?'

She ran the vein over a picture-hook and back again, lynching it finally over the doorhandle.

'See the film the other night? Japanese atomic monster. Waddling like a midget in a bag. To conquer mankind it lowered its head to stop the crowd, but it was a turtle and I would have just laughed wouldn't you? Honey?'

She was slipping out through the narrow gap in the doorway.

'I'll. I'll tell you a story. Darling? A tiny semtex man slept in the drawer of a matchbox, the back of his head polished. Right ageless he was. His head shrivelled like pantomime pants. Er . . . because he died, finally. And that's . . . not much of a story I realise, but.' The door clicked shut. 'You know what I mean – identity predators, razor massage, chin television, category mob, blue booze, trouble phone, brooding sheriff – follow me? Careful what you're doing out there babe. Babe?' I was alone and shouting now. 'So you're with me so far?'

The vein was tight as a carpline, drawing my skin like a tent. Would it hold?

And I remembered Eddie was due to drop round for the match. Would he be well enough to make it?

He was, and when he opened the door the whole apparatus pulleyed into gear, tearing at my cardiovascular system till my heart exploded through my chest and sli tugging along the floor like a landed fish. Ruby was long gone.

Got a call from her a year later. Asked where she was.

'I'm in a hotel, like I said I would be. I'm in a hotel stuffing the piano with dollars. Bombers add to the amusement of the view.'

Good old Ruby. Let nothing part the web in her grave.

The incident with the heart and all gave Eddie an idea – with the collapse of the gallery he'd been casting around for a new scam and this was an epiphany. Stole a huge aquarium and some blowfish, which gazed out at him as though expecting profundity or at least food. 'I'm sellin' these little beauties to hospitals and it's my pleasure.'

'Hospitals.'

'Yeah to use as blood pressure cuffs – look at this.' And he drew one out with a landing net. He stretched the fish, tying it round his upper arm and fastening it with string. 'Smashin',' he said, chuffed.

'So how d'you measure the blood pressure then?'

'Eh?'

'Where's the gauge, the accuracy Eddie?'

'Accuracy.'

Next time I entered the lab the aquarium was gone and not a word was said about it. Eddie was togged up in white. 'What you doing Eddie?'

'Analysing Bob's gob foam.'

'Is that wise?'

'Well for your information I've just discovered, rather too late, that it's not. See this luminous patch on the table? And the wood's eaten down, like? That's where I spilt some of the stuff. Call the fire brigade brother, or we're all of us good as dead.'

Then there was the cow jaw he swore would add ten

miles a gallon to the average family saloon. 'The mouth goes around in the gas tank, second to none.'

'Doing what?'

'Trick riding, stuff like that. Bubbles, that's what it's about. Had a mess of hard work killing the cattle.'

'So?'

'So . . . then.'

Bob got away with his crimes of course. Upon his release there was a dawn light shortening the shadows and this delighted him. Could it possibly be anything but dinosaurs over that hill?

'No dinosaurs,' he complained later. 'In fact, no one.'

'We were busy brother. Looking at the air.'

'Dinosaurs though eh? I bet you anything you like those mothers could talk.'

'To each other?'

'What else? To trees?'

'I talk to trees.'

'You're not a proper man.'

'Neither were they. And that's why they're gone forever.'

Surprisingly he and Eddie got together on a scam – Bob rigged up a puzzle with ignition caps and a timer. 'Sleep and the puzzle explodes.'

'And that's your idea of a marketable product.'

'It works.'

'So does my arse.'

'And haven't you sold that to one and all.'

The argument I pushed forth in my defence creaked as it exfoliated, so as a diversionary tactic I reminded Eddie of the time he'd tied his own arse to the back of a passenger train. He looked at me blank and unrepentant. 'Latching my arse to the train, I was dragged, slowly at first, then very fast, along the tracks.'

'I know you were. And what did you expect?'

'Something magical.'

'Magical. Like what?'

'A psychic protest of some kind. An eruption.'

'I suspect there was an eruption wasn't there, but not a psychic one. Are you the full shilling brother? In your head I mean? I mean nobody else does this.'

'No?'

'I'm telling you now brother so you'll know – nobody does this sort of lunatic crap, even if they're paid. Surely you suspected it wasn't normal?'

'Only when people in the stations started screaming and cutting off their screams almost immediately by clapping a hand over their mouth.'

'So they were letting out a single yelp in fact?'

'Yes.'

'Then the hand slammed over? Well by God brother you've learnt a lesson there. I say you've learnt one haven't you?'

'Yes brother. I've learnt that . . .' And he trailed away shamefully.

'Go on.'

He mumbled bashful, head bowed. 'I've learnt that a man must take his pleasure where he can.'

'I'm disappointed Eddie. Not for your sake, but for the sake of humanity. You're breathing its precious gases after all, you crude copy of a man. God must have laughed in your face as he made it. Hypodermic answers and panic jackets Eddie – expect nothing brighter.'

Eddie didn't respond to the gibe but I knew he was sharpening his knife – in his mind, you understand.

We didn't hear anything from Eddie for a few days and then the telegram.

BLIMP EXPLOSION STOP WISH YOU WERE HERE STOP EDDIE STOP

'You what?' I said, frowning at the telegram.

'Who cares brother? Who cares if he's lying, honest, alive or dead? Isn't it enough that he's not here?'

'I suppose so. Still . . .' I couldn't help wondering about the bastard's skill with a dagger. World class. That was the sort of fella we needed round here, in a fight. 'Listen I'll maybe go and see where this was sent from, be sure all's well.'

'You don't mean it do you?' Bob asked, sitting up in his deckchair. 'Why?'

'I'll be back.'

Turned out the telegram originated a snail's throw away – went round to Eddie's house and found him up a ladder, carving an endstood tree trunk into the shape of a tree. 'Crayfish totems lack the wingspread,' he said, without turning around.

'What's all this crap about an airship or something? What's happening in your mind?'

'Hollow kids' tickerclick innards of dust and spindle, muffled at the torso walls so as not to distract during sermons.'

'That's enough of that.'

'You asked,' he said, and turned toward me to show he was wearing some sort of knitted snout.

'A knitted snout eh?'

'Up to a point brother.'

'That's what I thought you'd say.'

And a knowing look from Eddie as if to say, we're

brothers truly, in secrecy and the embossed symbol of initiation. But I hadn't the faintest idea what he meant by it all.

I thought back to the balmy afternoons of someone else's youth – for convenience and pragmatism. Found one molecule of love. That was enough for me. Strength to go on.

'You'll make a green grave Eddie.'

'Eh?'

'Earlobes know the tomb is the enemy – killing soft flesh for the kick-off. The Reaper's gung-ho for earlobes brother. Think yours'd stick to his ribs eh? Don't be so sure. You'll plunge into hell without an ear or clue.'

'Ay?'

'Hell brother. The stairhead where you haven't a chance, a steamy swell greets you when you thought you were entering heaven, no revenge possible on the minister, make your selection amid garbage. Ah reward eh?'

'Not mine.'

'Oh, yes,' I assured him. 'A cartilage continent, raw bacon promise and mincemeat in a bed.'

I looked around the garden as Eddie continued chipping away. Telescopic vegetation. Interesting frequencies off the birds. Bushes dripping with saliva.

'So how was the devil?' Eddie asked. 'Surrounded by fawning demons surely?'

'Apparently that's all nonsense.'

'A pentangle then, on the floor.'

'I tried doing one but only managed that thing with an A inside. Went to church once though. People swallowed wafers and flipped resolve. Gods instantly looked in to contribute tears and terrifying music. Priest got to work and demanded love.'

'How did you react – with indifference or manipulation?'

'Started shaking in indignation and bliss. Embraced the traffic downtown after that.'

'Imagine you would. What's Bob up to?'

'Got himself a pet spine. Sort of serpent coiling off the table, you notice it and realise it's a . . .'

'A backbone.'

'Yeah.' I wondered what else to say. 'No harm there. What is it but a scalped back?'

'I suppose,' said Eddie, planing a branch. 'He should just be glad he saw the spine, really, followed its trail.'

'That's right, it seemed to have a mind of its own when he caught it. Which had to be removed of course. Otherwise it'd be . . . top-heavy.'

And that, in a nutshell, is why I consider myself more charming and worthy of life than Eddie, Bob, Fred or anyone else I know.

Trouble with the firing squad

'Fire!'

I saw with absolute clarity the bullets roar like missiles from their launchers and, with a split second to spare, slowed the course of time itself by imagining I was in the theatre watching a musical loved by all. Simultaneously I invoked the aid of the devil – which was easy as that's what I do anyway when in a theatre watching a musical loved by all. I'd barely begun and a fish head stuck out of space nearby. 'Who disturbs my rest?'

'Minotaur says you never rest.'

'You. Why do you call me?'

'It's these point 270 Winchester shells, your majesty. When they reach my perfect body they'll pause only a moment then it's curtains.'

So we struck a bargain – something about a life for a life, torment, bakery everlasting – and I rode away on him as though on a pantomime horse. The bastard smelt terrible.

'So you invoked the devil eh. Having entered hell earlier and stamped on his cat. You don't know where to draw the line do you brother?'

That was Minotaur Babs. In addition to his own voice he snickered a spare one out of each nose-barrel. These nostril-voices were evil. They addressed everyone as 'Sergeant', for a start. Then what they actually asserted: 'You're vermin Sergeant. A sickness. Look at you.' Nobody could take much of that babbling in stereo. His mouth-voice would just be ordering a pint in the meanwhile, all placid like. But he knew what was going on.

Purest night for sale in a window. He told me it was sentimental to put ideas into wakefulness. To what possible end? Identical paradigms tangle in life's endless equation.

I blurted something about doom and union.

'God and the opportunity to live divine beneath his perch eh? I expected better from you.'

'Well . . .'

'Underwear and signs pointing into the city was enough to distract the knights.'

'I get it Babs but—'

'Accordions disintegrate like dead lizards.'

'Needless to say—'

'Priorities brother. Wire anything, suffer enthusiasm, spoon guts from experts. Coins cool in the rainforests.'

I'd been watching Minotaur very closely, my senses whipping back and forth like an eel. In time I'd come to recognise pure fun and the worst pain of all as separate things. Before meeting him, the little understanding I'd garnered in my notes had all been about salad and torrential storms and I thought I'd seen everything. Minotaur consulted air. Streaks of inactivity striped him like a tiger.

'That bucket o' monkeys you consider a philosophy

won't hold together long brother. Where'd you get it anyway?'

'From a whore.'

'With a fridge full of guilt I suppose?'

Good old Minotaur. Airlock eyes and a brain of steel wool. Sectioned tail like an armadillo's. A class fiend for your money.

Meanwhile Eddie looked up to me. 'What happens at a circus brother?'

'The elephant's attention is claimed by a basketball, cymbals splash as the clowns attack, I weep for civilisation.'

'Don't you learn nuffin'?'

'Damage to me ears and no wisdom brother – feel I'm at school again. A cement mixer stopped and gone solid.'

'Will I ever be happy brother?'

'It'll end in a barrel-rolling frenzy of exploding glass and misfiring airbags Eddie – diagonally across the M21.'

'Not me.'

'Oh, yes. If I know the Reaper he'll be at you like a greyhound out of a trap.'

'Who's that then.'

'The Reaper – a bird of burden you might say.'

'Oh the Reaper eh? You're claiming to know him.'

'Claiming. I could introduce you.'

'Via a knife I suppose.'

'Not needed. Tonight I'll take you through the necessary wall – it'll push in like dough and then break, admitting us. Because we're fools.'

'Only fools go through then?'

'Only a fool'd want to.'

'So what did this Reaper have to say for himself then brother?'

'Asked him about death and the usual fare. The reason for it, you understand. You'll find his explanation as interesting as I did.'

'Count me in brother.'

The lights flickered. I don't recall which doomed revolution was occurring at the time but it played merry hell with the electricity supply.

That evening I stood holding to my belly a round mirror, ground and kept in the dark for this day. I'd bought another, larger one from the Shop o' Fury and Eddie swivelled this toward me to create a descending regression of images. Eddie peered at my midsection, squinting. 'I can see through a hole into another concern.'

'What do you see?'

'Weeds.'

'Are you sure?'

'As sure as I can be.'

'What else?'

'Eleventh-hour negotiations with a master chef.'

'Any other people?'

'Some U-boat captain in a polo-neck jumper.'

'That all?'

'I can see the boring mischief of a fez-wearing spider monkey in a Persian bazaar.'

'And?'

'A mirrorshaded and strenuously enigmatic chopper pilot.'

'Nothing more?'

'No, that's it.'

'Hardly worth the trouble then.'

'I know. But if we can just . . .'

And he stood around in front of the large mirror, letting go – it toppled slowly, falling over us. Blind displaced space.

No lamps, so we had to do the old match in the mouth trick. Bob always opted out in these situations as he was afraid we'd see he had no skull, only a sort of inverted basket made of cartilage. Of course I knew this from the moment I met him, having been trained by my aunt to assess people's heads in an instant. There was a pause as I went to shake his hand – I'm sure he noticed something wavering in my expression. But I never mentioned it then – a man's skull arrangements are his own affair, until he starts boasting.

Anyway me and Eddie started down these subterranean tunnels. A railing to hold, nothing else but dripping roofcracks and regular bulbs unlit and chemically flat. At intervals victims were still alive and held almost to the wall sighing or talking stories they thought made sense – pleasing nobody but themselves at last.

'What's this Reaper like then?' Eddie asked.

'Mate of John Satan. Angelically curtained in wrappings of human skin. Head in a bowling bag. Use your collarbone as a boomerang if you let him.'

'What makes you think I wouldn't.'

Upper sections of unease swayed over addiction deeps. Escarpments and thin floors led to the litter temple. On a glass throne the Reaper sorted dazed chains, surrounded by a retinue of blade angels.

'What happens here?' Eddie whispered.

'Darkplan wars – success when nobody returns.'

The delicate balcony gave way, rolling us into the temple. The Reaper turned its hollow iron head. 'Yes?'

'Sorry to disturb you my lord. Thought I'd pop by and ask you to fry the rind of me ligaments.'

'I'll give you a dull pain in good remains. Days gone dead in the iris. Best I can offer.'

'That's how they are here,' I whispered to Eddie. 'Talk in front, blood-lust at the rear.' Then I spoke up to the Reaper. 'That your final word, corky? Surely you could think of something fiercer for my friend here.'

'The iron thought thinks not. In heaven darkness is an opportunity for privacy and escape.'

'See what I mean?' I asked Eddie in an undertone. He just stared agog at the bladers' thin splitting skin and the polished nightbirds sniggering with need. 'All right biff,' I told the Reaper, coming over elaborately indifferent. 'But just don't try rippin' us off okay?'

Trundling reality rocked aside and allowed entrance to a garrison of torment I've since come to know as a home from home. At least it makes no bones about what it is. Sometimes I'd be tied down and tortured till my belly split releasing elms, anglers, ants, dogs, hosepipes, jets of flame, lengths of velvet, stoplights, fruit, bones, gods, broken staves, betting slips, trolls, dartboards, popcorn, sharks, antlers, panicking chefs, scarves, busts of Lenin, barnacles, haranguing beggars and billowing clouds of buff-coloured smoke. Of course I'd become so bored I'd start whistling and playing the fool.

'He's whistling,' said one torturer, indignant.

'Better than nothing,' said another philosophically.

'So how did you like it?' I asked Eddie afterwards, slapping him on the back. 'Sundrenched and frying jelly in the stove of your head – holiday and a half.'

'Sounds good.'

'Good? We've just been there. And it's damnation.'

'Call it what you like, it's better than what I've known.'

Now, of course, life's lash is fully unfurled from the nursery branch. I don't need to purchase trouble. But I sleep well. Night's a paperweight holding my alsation

and me like two suicide notes to a freemason's desk.
Unachieved, my destiny drums its bony fingers as I snore.
So, doc – what do you make of it?

Trouble with the shrink

'This is *without* drugs?'

At least that's what he'd been chanting earlier. Then he'd started brandishing a norm grid at the onward flow. Thought the core stick symbolised a cock but got everything else wrong. Didn't believe in the existence of a being called 'Eddie', for starters. 'How do you sense his presence?' he asked at one point, still humouring me. Bloody good question though.

Now, of course, my face was the venue for a punching bonanza. He shouted all kinds of slogans – 'You'd *say* all that would you?' – that sort of thing. Alternately jabbing his finger at the wall-clock and my eyes. Really puce and angry as I scrabbled to leave. Had to kick him in the balls finally, slamming out as he bent over, face turning reflex blue.

On the way back, pulled over. Had me arm hung out casual like. Copper acting hard and refusing to look at me – staring off down the road as he flipped his notebook. 'The road talks to herself,' he said.

'I know that.'

'You're a cool one.'

'Let me articulate both my snouts or I'll be neglecting communion.'

'I'll ignore that remark sir.'

'At my edges, yolk runs like an aura.'

'Now that's enough of that—'

'Unburied victims await you in a cluster, rooms red with new vintage.'

'What? What you . . . er now don't move—'

'My mistress hammers anything helpless and no recall – inaccuracy sneers at the true bard.'

'Don't move a muscle you bastard—'

'Spider crash, spider crash – the old shelf falls.'

'Don't *say* that!'

'Heaven's vertebrae are damn near impossible – lymph and paraffin alternate in that there kingdom.'

'Quiet now you—'

'Dogs nurture an ideal – and are ready to report.'

'No!'

'I have boiled money.'

'Get – get—'

'Chains quarried from cold teeth.'

'Get out of here!'

'Thank you officer.'

Went to coast – walked on beach. Gull wobbled in the air like a memo caught in a spiderweb. Pity the pet fish which has a name – Tony, or Pluto – right between the eyes. Then whatever it does will be seen as evidence of rueful personality – look at Tony, his fins unfurled, near the airbubbles. Look at Pluto, collecting the fishfood in his face. Hell in such a small space.

Rested my face and ears on a bartop in a tavern on the bay. Slow ceiling fan, wooden shutters, smoke, there's the style. Key West. Irritable exiles. Shabby intrigue.

Guy in a captain hat held an entire pig in front of his open mouth, and paused.

'First of the day,' he said.

Then the violence. He noticed my look after a while. 'What? Rather I ate elsewhere? With a man's face brought along for a napkin? Pick out summer from a picnic and you're left with idiots in a marsh.'

He pulled a trotter out of his nose.

'Trends end here and crash, young man, bursting like empty bubbles, leaving no wreckage – honesty at the last, baking us all. Deny this and get my furled hand in your belly like a bird come home to roost. Think otherwise? The drains here feed directly into my windpipe. The graveyard's poppied with maggots, ribs serve as a slot for daggers, sense is beat all to pudding and I'm glad. Look there.' He pointed at the wine-rack, which was arrayed with fist-size grubs. 'A country mile from what you'd expect isn't it? But I'm telling you it's the gutter norm. What's life in this nation? Collect emptiness in a household of cornflakes. Transient fuel gobbles attention, the television aches, the truth walks. Scheme worms welcome your corpse, trap clicks and you're in heaven, bored rigid. Eh?'

'I s'pose.'

'You s'pose? How old are you? Me I'm broken on the rack of me own heartbeat, you've still got friends to twist into accidents. That's it boy, example the only souvenir, take it or leave it – then consolidate and warp.'

'Warp.'

'All you got to do is go overside – get ribs instead of hair. Ask the earth its long name. Damn it, creatures snorted in battle right here sonny. Triceratops always got his first. That despite the horns. And the armour, my God. Take that to a court of law and see how fair life can be.'

He slammed his fist at a space-insect on the bar, turning it to glue.

'They use dinosaurs round here for pleasure – oh you don't have to believe that. Or anything I've said, why should you? Just promise you won't come over here later asking for a good servicing. I'll pretend I don't know you – or anything. So what do you say young man?'

'What's that you're drinking sir?'

'This dayglo stuff, see?'

'What is it?'

'Propellant.'

'Propellant?'

'For a vertical-take-off jet. Can't say fairer than that.'

'I have to go now.'

'Uh? But we're just gettin' friendly.'

'Bye now.'

'Hey – hey you with the gristle badge! Come back here!'

Found I couldn't leg it as fast as I was used to. 'The cramps are caused by other people's shite ideas wedging into your flow modality,' said the doctor. 'Eat lots of fruit and tell anyone who comes near you to piss off and die.'

'Cigarette?'

'Don't mind if I do. That's a cigarette box full of recriminations isn't it?'

'Yes.'

'Thought so. You know you're a very complex man. How do you do it?'

'Dachshund gymnastics.'

'Get out.'

I got more and more concerned that there was nothing wrong with me. Oriental surgeons tutted about the size of my eyes. 'Do you always stare like this?' said the English-speaking one.

'Only when someone else is picking up the cheque,' I said, and watched him relay this to his colleagues. Startled, they immediately began jabbering and shoved me from the operating table in a clatter of cutting tools. 'How come?' I protested, pointing at the main man. 'He's upgraded to nightmare guard and I'm snubbed even as mascot.'

That put the true frighteners on them.

I approached the local chemist with the words 'Pharmaceutical friend, we meet once again in the wrinkled throat of stacked odds', and that was the end of it. Barred – and doubts whispered as quiet as the split of a hair as they chased the windblown petal of profit. That and my staring in through the shrink's window the other time and him getting terrified at the very least, as I whispered near-inaudible: 'The first impulse to life is a mistake we spend the remainder regretting – acrid knowledge of death's throat, bats when they are hidden, snakes and their unpredictability, giraffes with their eyes a-shining. These are all my enemies, blotting my horizon and whining without interlude. When my ship comes in it'll be skippered by a bastard and crewed by trolls. Aft and fore braces betagged with the ears of spaniels and sails patched with the flesh of ministers. Antennae the lash and dung the cargo. Remember it.'

Told the others later in the bar.

'Beat them off single-handed eh?' said Minotaur. 'Step ghastly brother – you've ear-to-ear arrogance going so light.'

'Wish I could do that,' said Eddie, thoughtful.

Bob heard this and went bananas. 'Your mouth swallows a regular salary of air doesn't it? Vegetation adjusts around your way? So you exist.'

'Leave him alone brother,' I laughed amicably. 'Change

of image, that's the way. Mask and a chainsaw might be just the thing. Think about it Eddie.'

'A trash-wading angel uninfluenced by effluvia eh?' Bob snorted scornfully, and I felt entirely justified in ignoring him. 'And I suppose that trip to hell with Eddie was a laugh too? Who ever heard of a Pre-Raphaelite interrogation?' Driven by a conviction which was nearing the end of its life, he offered to beat my head off completely.

'When in doubt lash out eh Bob? You don't face perfection seeing, so much as talking, challenging and worsening your heart. That's not the fine way brother. We are in the midst of an intense heat, the very dogstar of subterfuge. And I gasp with laughter in a tyre-rim factory. Chum, I'm stood here the risen Christ. A cigarette in each nostril, I save time for myself and others. Clams yawn like a garbage truck as I approach with an opener. The embassy summon me and call me *bastardo*, slapping my face with my own passport. A filament of butterfly nerve anchors my virtues.'

'Your rain autographs our streets with disappearing ink is that right?' rumbled Bob. 'You're a charlatan's what you are.'

'You say I'm a charlatan eh?'

'That's what I said you bastard now make me understand why you think otherwise.'

'You assume I think otherwise.'

'You do don't you? – you do or you're pure evil.'

'I am evil. I make a point and show of it for those with the smarts to confront what I'm up to.'

'Up to. You admit there's underhandedness included in all this.'

'Oh yes. Underhandedness, murder – and lethargy, heaps of a particular brand of lethargy.'

'Heaps of lethargy you say. A particular brand. All right you bastard now that I've kept you talking this long here are the police – you can explain all your nonsense to their dead faces. Didn't expect that now did you? Afternoon, officer – called you about this bastard here – talking shite and wasting my sweet time.'

'Evening Fred.'

Trouble with the priest

'So Empty Fred swans in all togged out like a copper then, is that the song you're trying to sing now.'

'Yes.'

'You're persisting with that one are you?'

'Told you he was a dab hand. Then Godber's Troops landed naked in the precinct and started shouting at startled bargain-hunters.'

'And what were the Troops shouting?'

' "I just want to be left alone." And I ran. Because the Lobster Academy were after me.'

'I see.'

'You know what I mean when I say the Lobster Academy were after me.'

'You mean everyone.'

'Ten out of ten Sonny Jim – good for you. And I collided with a martyred clown who had steam smoking out of a vertical mouth slot. My head rested on the martyr's shoulder and shone like a brothel lamp. Initially poison is quite relaxing, as you'll know.'

He let out a strange gasp. 'I can't quite believe it. You think that to parley with demons is a matter for laughing?

The plumcake of trauma you call a childhood has left you with a coinbiting distrust of reality.'

'Not really padre. Just bored rigid. Luckily that's the style round here so nobody notices.'

'You consider yourself normal?'

'Doesn't everyone's cock have a ribcage?'

He took a deep, hostile breath. Then the judgement. 'You'll end spooning out eyes and embalming bodies for company brother.'

'That's an interesting point padre – yes I—'

'Dangerous man. Knife poised at the belly of this community. How can you live with those snakes a-squirm in your head? It makes me shiver to think—'

'—now that's all very well padre but will you—'

'—somehow able to operate in this world despite a burden of evil which would prostrate a concrete ape.'

'—will you hear my confession or not you bastard?'

A fist splintered through the partition and the entire yammer box began to topple amid our own screams and those of the bastards queuing outside. He got out of his door but mine was facing the floor and they left me there 'to burn'. That's what they thought. In fact I'd brought some lard in with me, so there was plenty of fun to be had.

Anyway I got the film developed but while I was off doing that Eddie had given up on the underlab and tried to get a proper job – told us all about it afterwards. He handed the interviewer a CV consisting of sketches of tortoises. 'There you go,' he said, handing it over, 'get your choppers round that.'

'Tell me, how do you see your future?'

Eddie knew this question was coming and had a little speech prepared. 'The future is something to answer for in bureaucratic voices. Bureaucratic voices after all, tones of belief and eyes that sparkle, in my life these are like love. The future? Metallic breathing under old skies. Mutant maps, the reflection of the city on the beach. Pinhole ears, pinhole philosophy. The future. The future is ours.'

'That's . . . a very original, and I venture to say, heartening view. What are your present circumstances?'

'Contagious cats, infested ruin.'

'And what do you see as your greatest asset?'

'I'm completely blameless.'

'Have you ever considered your face?'

'Never.'

'Your face is much more important than you give it credit for. I have here a dozen reports that it's worth fifty-two grand. I was going to grant you anything you like but I can't possibly now. No, we're sending you into space Eddie.'

'Space? Why?'

'Upon re-entry you'll scare citizens off the streets and I'll be able to go my way in peace for once.'

'Would you excuse me a minute?'

And he ran as fast as his arms and legs would take him.

Eddie's mesmeric inability to behave like a man had us on the floor laughing. 'Corner-slumped in a stark bathroom Eddie, digesting hair and cosmetics. There's your end, oh yes, I know it now.'

'You don't.'

'Grinding to the public as privacy gets a busy signal eh Eddie?'

'Not me.'

And he tried again, down in the lab. Growing a waiter this time. By the light of a single bare bulb its cocoon was anything but suspicious. In the protoplasm its resistance diminished in drags of chemical soporific. Some claimed there was a nursery especially for this kind of larval and sometimes violent transformation, and helpers to clear away the slime. Don't you believe it. If anything like that existed it'd be a multimillion industry, not a cottage concern.

I was sat in the lab alone when it began to wake, pushing at the embryo. But when it birthed in a burst of aftermilk it was so like a real waiter I kicked it in the balls and then bashed its head in with a rock. I was still killing it when Eddie came in and saw the mess.

'Well Eddie,' I panted, straightening up, 'as you can see, fractures went right across his face like a window hit by a stone.'

'What caused that then?'

'His face was hit by a stone – and you know why.'

'Tell me.'

'Because he asked for it.'

'In words?'

'Not in words, no – by his acts and his knowledge of their inevitable consequence. Everyone knows that.'

'Perhaps he didn't.'

'I can assure you everyone knows it.'

'Okay brother. Now about this broken face, how did it happen?'

'Didn't I just get through explaining this to you in all finery?'

'Yes so you did. Could this by any stretch be the life-for-a-life the devil swore you to when you dodged the firing squad?'

'Fat chance Eddie – but let's call the coroner to give it the stamp of authenticity eh? Maybe old John Satan'll think it's pukka.'

Strains attended the death photograph of its blue

frightened face – bones like hotdogs twisted its calm, its wrists mangled, hounds' teeth and other hardware left in its throat. A rolled rug was found up its arse. Powdered gold wafted from some quarter. The whole procedure was baffling and awkward. 'That the end?' asked the Mayor.

'Yes,' said the photographer, packing up quickly.

'Thank God – what a tragedy for this talented man, let's get out of here.'

And I thought, how little we know, how little we *really* know about our innards.

So once again we'd escaped the law – that and the berserking apes were the glue which could hold an arrest together. But I can't pretend I'd forfeit my memory of seeing those chimps in action. Afterwards I remember saying hats were something to hold us up. That's how disorientated their mayhem left me – flumming my arms like a 'copter. Trying to whistle and speak at the same time.

Then the nightmares. Heavily manacled and bowed with laudanum, I summed up my case – presented with head on plate, rude to refuse, music and agreeable company. Deny everything Eddie says, grabbing my arm an instant before the police burst in. Into the fire with remains as doors explode. Shame hailers, dollar physics and invented memories. And I woke with a yell – one of the best of its kind I ever heard.

Went to consult Bob on the meaning. Looked around his place. 'What's in the boxes Bob – graveyard earth?'

'I have devoted my room to yapping statistics.'

'What are these?' I asked, crouched at the skirting board.

'Dignity vents.'

'All right Bob enough suspense – what does the dream mean? The head on the plate?'

'You've grown heads brother – you know.' And he explained. That sense of power which was so much a part of head-eating as though at an egg in the morning, the head's face bleary and slack in after-death, was so boring to me that I forgot it as soon as it was described. Bob had built it up as the great mystery and this is all it was. 'And don't ever touch the face of a sheep,' he said ominously.

'Should I let a sheep touch my face?' I asked flippantly, and laughed at his glaring. Narrow groove in his forehead making me understand he didn't care for my talk of tender love.

'Ah you're the rare thing brother,' said Minotaur at the shop. 'Larging it up and lamping the old bill with their own hammers. There's the true way.'

'Well thank you brother,' I said, and with his sudden stare it dawned upon me that he meant to condemn.

'Poisoned or bludgeoned brother – make your choice.'

'Neither.'

'No time nor space for that,' he replied, forcing beetles into his pipe and striking a match. The bugs popped and crackled when lit. 'Fear for man if you think furnaces are final. Poisoned or bludgeoned?'

'Those are the choices eh?'

'Hell yes.'

'Give me a moment. Poisoning or bludgeoning. I don't get it.'

'It's simple. You're in the way.'

'But why the restricted options Babs? I hope you don't think I'm a low priority.'

'Oh I feel a deep respect for you – surely you know this.'

'I am trying. I'm trying to know it, but here I am

between a rock and a hard place brother – poisoning or some kind of . . . repeated blows is it?'

'Flies don't hesitate.'

'Eh? Oh look you'll have to decide for me I – I can't.'

'Very well.'

Toys rushed in, snarling to eat.

Three hours later I staggered into the bar, clothes shredded.

'What happened?'

'Robot,' I gasped. 'Face like a smoke alarm. Came in shouting. All I remember.'

'Must have made the transition to an injured and unconscious man,' said Fred.

'Where were you?' asked Bob.

'Shop o' Fury.'

'Oh, Minotaur's harmless as a scorpion in a paperweight – you must have had a bad dream.'

I was about to put a match to the nail bomb of my opinions when Eddie entered and, in a surge of ambition, tried introducing us to someone who wasn't himself. It was one of Godber's Troops, who rode in on the following remark:

'I'm Mister – J-J-J-J-J-Jesus!'

'You all right?'

'Bloody bastard convulsions – back again! Ah!'

'Jesus fucking Christ.'

'Ah-ah-ah – J-Jesus! F-f-f-k-k-J-J-j-j-j-j-k-j-k-k-k-l-k-k-!'

'Get this bastard out of here,' I yelled, 'and get me a drink of water.'

'What about his convulsions brother?' shouted Empty Fred.

'An electrical tossing and pact with the situation of flapping when you least expect it.'

'I know what it *is* – what to *do* about it brother? He'll break furniture wherever he is.'

'Their owners will worry.'

'That's what I'm *saying* brother.'

'Incarceration. Or taming in a cage with whip and chair? Torture? Who am I?'

'Are you all right brother?'

'I'm saving my ideas for a time when everything will be perfect to receive them. I'm absolutely amazing.'

'*What?*'

'Stand aside.'

'*What?*'

'I'm an angel with twelve hours to go.'

'He's cracked his lid. *Bob! Eddie! Help!*'

'Charming the daylight out of the bloody trees.'

'*Eddie! Bob! Brother! Brother!*'

Beautiful convulsions – world class.

Anyway lads, the aliens started as they meant to go on, boring everyone rigid with their birthcries. Who could have predicted we'd look back on our loneliness so wistfully? The old haycart pastorals are full of spaceships and dogs are flattened by landing pads. And if we look closely at the telltale prong pattern, here, and here, I think we can establish categorically that this is not a pig, but a spaniel and incidentally yes, I did kill it.

Trouble with every last bastard in the bar

The bar was a frozen tableau of indignation and resentment. Educated perhaps in the terrifying arts, the barman was silent. Fleets of ants carried away my resolve. Empty Fred was still stood with his hand outstretched and petalled with betting stakes. Now he furled this hand upon the cash and used the resultant fist to smash my expression.

I knew, the way you do, that it was time to run. And my face began to bubble like a soup, erupting with bone and prowing out, until I was transfigured into an old lady.

'Gawd blimey I'm saved,' I gasped, and laughed with relief.

But absolutely everyone had witnessed the transformation, and so my powers of disguise were rendered useless. My only hope was pity.

But fists soon fidget. Surrounded by kicking wasters, my limbs instinctively adopted defence formation. The priest, above all, bitterly contested my version of events, saying I should 'curb my mouth', whatever that means. Oh my brothers it's a fine thing when the most we can hope for is a kick upside the face from a saviour. An American laugh track was being played over the speakers throughout the procedure. I'll teach these little Hitlers to play hardball, I thought, bursting into tears. Freaked shadows leapt up the wall, of many bastards ganging up on one. Which is unlawful, by the way.

Protocol demanded defeat but I was getting louder, gasping sarcasm mixed with gob blood. 'What's next for you Eddie? What'll you do? Rip off a gran and piss the proceeds up a wall surely.'

'Eh?'

'Sliced canopy, flies, empty flask – there's your end.'

'Not me,' he said, pausing mid-punch to describe a plan for inflicting tiles on the roof of his gaff. As it continued Eddie's explanation for his purpose in life relinquished its slender claim to coherence. All fists turned to him. Run our boy, run.

I found a bench upon which to mend and tilled over what I'd learnt about the pitfalls of bleating. Almost every visit to the pub went horribly, tragically wrong. I really appreciated this. Put your hands over your face if you want to protect it but you miss so much – memory markers, current gates rampant, springloaded opinions, wrecked filter. Nothing shut the bastards up anyway.

I don't know what anyone else leaves for protection money but I left the evidence of my leisure, an airy and insubstantial thing you'd need a scholar to verify, and when the criminal fraternity dragged me out of a kennel and told me not to scream too loudly, it was clear they thought I'd bequeathed them nothing at all. Three more sacrifices were added to the many with which my life was draped – four hours of my time, one pint of blood for each of those hours, and the age-old horror of having my wisdom and charm fall upon small, deaf ears. Left me nervy – cigarette and double-takes at glimpsed spiders, you know.

The meaningful form and pattern of spilt blood was what decided most arguments back then, as now. That and toxicology – Minotaur for instance was a toxicology adept. Though he'd fart like a sailor and stamp on elves when he saw them – and only he did – you couldn't help but respect the man. Arguments raged about his age and the number of terms he would have served if there were any justice, and he himself named the top figure, laughing aloud and buying beer for all in the winter bar. Minotaur was a depth charge everyone waited on, ready for the spectacle.

When Minotaur fought it was hard to recognise the fact. It involved hurled occult curses and the puffing of blowdarts, an occasional overturned cauldron or spilt prayer. Shrieks were in Latin and frilled in finery such as—

'Smoke makes windows black as horses and sweetness is everywhere attacked.'

—upon being hit unexpectedly by a thrown chair.

Anyway I had my revenge by inviting every last bastard to a 'disguise yourself as a normal fella' party. I let out one confidential laugh then admitted the guests – as I typed, smoked, perched like a bird on my dog's head and made up a list of names deserving penance in the cellar with dry taps. All uncomprehending, they lamely closed the door on their freedom.

I knew from a test I'd done with Eddie that two weeks was the sheer maximum I could leave bastards without food and at the end of that time I went to the locked door sniggering and chirped 'Do the bastards want to come out now?'

'Yes,' came the cry all feeble like.

'Say it all.'

'The bastards want to come out.'

'Oh you do now,' and so on till they spent their final strength in rage. Then I threw the old bolt and their eyes squinted upward, along with a few gun muzzles – all credit to 'em they were prepared.

My life is glued with such afternoons, keeping morons at bay with empty threats and praying for gullibility, or instantly returning bricks which had crashed into my silent front room with a flick of the curtain. I grew into a man and these circumstances subsisted like a rockery.

Eventually had to make my peace with the neighbourhood by the giving of gifts. To Eddie I took a tangle of snot.

'What's that?'

'Nose-born reptile. Put it here – overhanging the drain okay?'

To Bob an initialled lighter in the shape of a cheap lighter and a bed stuffed with tobacco.

To Empty Fred a wall clock which transformed into millions of rabbits aglow and a gilded invitation to sample 'the immortal caviar of God's brain'. He declined.

To Minotaur a branding iron and vodka, and to Carver – who wasn't involved in the feud and not aware really of anything – fourteen sorry words.

To the Mayor I couldn't be arsed to give anything and he cursed me, bursting into tears like a girl.

To the priest a locust.

When these duties were complete I immediately resumed hostilities. Astonished everyone by treading on the face of a snail and remembering every feature of it, to the point where I had detailed nightmares in which the creature was a bewigged judge. Me in the dock accused of sizzling with enlightenment or something.

'State your name.'

'Identity yeah, not so fast. Oi judge, you hate the crusts eh, me too. A beak and vertebrae, that's all you need – no offence yer honour, I mean a bill. Not the old bill I mean, oh gawd I'm makin' a right bollocks outa this. Bill of a bird I mean – feathered variety that is, oh gawd . . .'

'Would you describe the black events of the night in question?' or something like that.

'I'm glad you had the smarts to ask – better than stinking in wedlock at a lousy address eh? All started at this big do. Love a party me. If good smooth banisters support me I'll be there, drawing attention. A friend sounded odd and I realised he was waiting for money. Skin me mind. So that night nipping from a haunted sleep to the bog, saying soggy prayers and playing spiritual billiards, know what I mean. Gored by a bull – wait a minute, by a big bull – and bam did the lawyers arrive, smoke from me heart as I breathed deeply. Chicken doctors visited, called me mate, bedspread world, all that. No I ain't finished yet.'

And I was being dragged out shouting.

'One grave's enough for me milord. Keep all me identification fingers on one hand, know what I mean. See you soon baby. Me door's always open – and me roof. Treasure creosote, ladies and gentlemen, treasure it.'

Told Bob about the dream and he thundered low. 'Do you enjoy making the rest of us feel stupid?'

'Yes brother.'

'And what gives you, of all people, the authority?'

'Meat stairs led to the charm school. That's *my* excuse anyway, ha. Get the glint out your eye and give it here so I can pay the bus home, ha ha.'

Even Bob's got his little routines. Every few months he sloughs off his skin, leaving only the head part because he's embarrassed about the odd condition of his skull, you know. 'So long as it grows back,' he laughs, 'I'm a new man.' And it really is the only thing which enlivens him. 'You should try it brother. Slowly, mind.'

I was so unaware of my appearance I didn't feel the proper terror. Yes I was immature, with the luxury of health.

After peeling myself I was redder. Pepper face.

'Didn't I just tell you at massive cost to human life to go slowly?' shouted Bob aghast, and added I may yet be all right – only time would tell. Scared the bejesus out of me till I healed. God the relief – once again souped up with skin.

Bob's nerve beard was growing apace. But in time he forgot his achievement and went to shave, instantly shrieking with an agony as new and bright as the morning beyond his window.

Sacred isn't the word for Bob's views. Assail them and you'll find a machine-gun tower posted at his mind-edge. Can't be bought for love or mud that man and if you try he'll belt you with your own uprooted leg. Went to see him once and he was biting the wall. 'Tough room,' he said, and pulled, inverting a corner and dragging a cone of matter toward us. Reality started screaming. Something about its rights.

'Knock it off brother,' I said nervously.

Bob didn't hear, tugging at the continuum like a suckling babe. 'That's right that's right that's right,' he seemed to say through his teeth, which were throwing sparks. He shouted suddenly and the room took the opportunity to snap back into place like a bastard caught rifling a drawer.

Bob sank back chuffed and exhausted. 'I love a wrecked dream don't you?' he said.

'I can't understand where your insides end and the rest starts.'

'You've told me before,' he said dismissively, but in too good a mood to strike out. And he called this a 'saving grace'.

That evening I was draped over a chair and flailing my arms, learning to swim. Eddie walked in. 'What you doing brother?'

'Attempting to salve the threatening sensation Eddie.'

'Answer through a window brother.'

'Stemming shortcuts Eddie.'

'Notice how the answer changed?'

'So what.'

'Well don't you consider it strange?'

'Possibly.'

'Aren't you interested even?'

'I can take or leave it.'

And as the day was defeated and fell again to forgetting the lesson in that event, we stood and spectated.

'Just look at that sunset brother – red as a windburned pig.'

'Shepherds take fright brother.'

'Looks like a furnace.'

'Or a grated salmon.'

'Or a drunkard's exploding eye.'

'Or a mime caught in the glare of a truck's headlights.'

'Or a chum-line for taunting sharks.'

'Or a giant enjoying a coronary.'

'Unbeatable.'

Eddie knelt and lifted a rock. 'Lawyers,' he whispered.

Trouble with the police

'When you're ready then.'

'Eh?'

'I'm waiting.'

'What for?'

'This alleged explanation you moron.'

'Well this was it.'

'When?'

'Just now. The dogs, the charm, all that.'

'Ah. Oh I see.' He looked down at his notes, turning a couple of pages back and forth. 'So you expect me to believe this scenario do you sir?'

'You think I could make this up? For God's sake I was informed on by a badger, how credible is that? You'd believe him before you'd believe me?'

'Frankly, yes.'

'I can't believe I'm hearing this.'

He looked at me, face careworn. 'You think I find it easy slipping my hooks into perpetrators little by little?'

'Piece of piss. Someone strangles your car – suspects line up, all with big hands. "Turn around." Everything else is small. "Smile." Their smiles are small. "Perform a strangling motion." They do so – and one repeats his smile. Bingo.'

'Bingo eh? Bob's your uncle just like that.' He paused a while, considering. 'Allow me to show you something Sonny Jim.'

He led me through strange airless spaces of museum boxes, radio heaters and telephone rooms, dark colleges heaving in the windows.

'Look here,' he said, opening a door into a small walk-in closet. All manner of confiscated shite on the shelves – pizza, badly preserved guilt and muddy skulls. 'Guilt and pizza, well they're a luxury aren't they, but try living without your skull. Eh? See where that gets you.'

'I agree, so what.'

'Just simple rules,' he said, with meaning. 'There's a rule not to go in carving an ornament which is already completed. Stands to reason – a thing's on fire, what's all that about? Put it out. And then there's this.' Reaching up, he took a scrap of paper from a high shelf, handed it over and leaned at me, his face as waxen as a fetish saint. He watched with jaundiced eyes as I read it.

' "On a ship of games, the dice clacked with fear." What like the boat was full of gamblers and that set the course? What's sinister about that? Keys up a flagpole – *that's* sinister. Boxes of teeth, but this? Put a window in it and yeah I'll grant you – oh get out of it you're ridiculous.'

I pushed past him and stormed out of the place – he ran up the drive booming, 'You'll get what's arriving! And I don't mean that pisspoor little insurance bonfire in Epping Forest neither boy! You're headed for the tall one!'

Went round Eddie's.

'Coming to the pub Eddie? Where's Empty Fred?'

'Core creatures globed out of the wall and gripped him by the shoulders, dragging him backward into a hell which was screeching for his blood.'

'Well we can't hang about – come on.'

'Core creatures though.'

'Of course core creatures Eddie.'

'Big ones mind. Teeth like toilet bowls brother.'

'Now you simmer down there.'

'Stroking the whole way down the cat and talking the sinister talk, you know. What they'd do to me.'

'Sure Eddie.'

'All calm about it like.'

'I know the way.'

'Then up they stood and charged me.'

'How much was that then?'

'Not greenbacks brother – ran at me when I least expected it to happen. That's what the previous behaviour was for – to prepare the ground for the subsequent abominations.'

'Sharp relief you mean.'

'That's what I believe.'

'So when they charged you were taken all unawares. Did you call for assistance?'

'Yes. And more of them arrived.'

'What took place Eddie – spare me no finely crafted detail.'

'There was a lake of blood in the front room. Well not a lake but—'

'I know what you mean.'

'And I was concerned. So there was a chiming and I saw the clock was turned so the hands resembled a man wrecking his own chances.'

'You think Fred had left a message.'

'He was the sort of amateur to do that wasn't he? Conspiring among eternity. No size in confusion.'

'I've seen this happen before. The creaks and clicks of a growing face gave way to bangs and a kind of thundering grind. Primal machinery of horror. Associates get shit-scared. Fred becomes a marked man without understanding.'

'I wasn't scared.'

'Oh your secret's safe with me brother.'

'So I went to the pond. Fish-shaped animals were swimming in the water.'

'I think you'll find those were fish Eddie.'

'That's your opinion is it? Were they now? Well you can keep your opinions in a cool dry place brother. Because these were speaking to me with their mouths.'

'You're sure they weren't carp Eddie?'

'Not carp brother. And they said I was the Chosen One and had to go down unto the Hound and thereby meet an Emissary of some kind.'

'Greyhound in Bromley?'

'That's how I understood it.'

'And you did this?'

'Of course not, are you mad? Wouldn't be caught dead in Bromley.'

'Well that's a story and a half there Eddie, I feel better – enlightened you might say.'

'That was the hope brother.'

So the old hoofer had taken Empty Fred for me sins – uncalled for or what. I couldn't understand why John Satan had such a downer on me anyway – could have sworn I hadn't used the mirror from Eddie's gallery again. Of course I later realised Eddie sold it to Minotaur, who put it in the Shop o' Fury, from which I purchased it for the purpose of taking Eddie to see the Reaper. There's one to tell the grandchildren. What's more it turned out Eddie was blandly aware of it all but didn't understand the significance of this or anything.

Thought I'd consult Minotaur. 'Don't interrupt when I'm drilling,' he said, aghast as I entered. He was holding down a struggling hen.

'I suppose you call this a service to mankind.'

'So what do you call it?'

'Cowardice – that mammal can't fight.'

'Mammal? Are you mad?'

'Lizard then – anyway it's just a small bastard you've probably taken by surprise is what I mean.'

'I've been talking about it to this little beauty for weeks – haven't I love?'

The hen looked up mournfully.

'There – are you reassured now brother?'

'Yes – of your madness.'

'Ha ha – nice one.'

'Anyway the reason I'm here is old Fred – been assaulted by his own structure.'

'Core creatures eh? Can't say I'm altogether surprised. That bastard's been flirting with danger for months.'

'How d'you mean?'

'I'll show you.'

Dropping the hen into a steel barrel, he slammed the lid and went over to the furnace. The heat when the hatch swung open was unbelievable. Plunging a pair of industrial tongs into the blaze, he carefully retrieved a cinder the size of a hubcap and perched it on an anvil. As the smoke cleared, I detected in the charred surface the embossed face of Fred's mother. 'What's this got to do with anything?'

'It's a cake,' said Minotaur, offended. 'For Fred's birthday.'

'When?'

'Last year some time.'

'Last year? What are you on about? Why are you wasting my time? What the bloody hell's been going on in here with that hen, where is it?' I grabbed the hen out of the barrel. 'Look at the poor bastard.'

'I know. Beautiful isn't she.'

'You sick fuck,' I said. 'Mind you she's not bad.'

In truth, she was adorable. Why hadn't I seen it before? I had to get her out of here – be alone with her.

'Er listen brother – I know you'll be straining at the leash to rescue Fred from the clutches of the devil and so on – I'll take care of the hen for you, er . . . my pleasure honestly.'

'I'll wager it would be,' he replied, fixing me with a caustic stare. 'Killjar brothers date their dreams, the horizon wounds like a knife, pebbles surge in roil-whispers – and other calculated marvels. Don't try bullshitting me, brother.'

So I went through again, compounding everything with another use of the flux glass.

Found my way to a sort of whirlpool of red guts, ectoplasmic though so it didn't stain my shirt or anything. The devil was there, face like a bag of spanners, gills venting red. And the Reaper – there grinned its head, spokes for teeth, all that. They were playing cards on the floor, absorbed. Fred looked round, blistered in egg machinery. 'Ceremony – don't look.'

'Seen it all before brother. What happened to you?'

'Core bastards. Fangs vivid with innocence rent and whatnot. Carpeted room with rubber, carved grid on heart, savoured screams then off. And look at me in my new permutation of agony brother.'

Fred's bone career was reaching a crescendo – he was so convolute he looked like a sea-drenched ammonite.

'Yeah. Local morality's bifocal.'

'Tell me about it – really crude.'

'Always has been. Fixed menu.'

'Even here.'

'Yeah, disappointing isn't it?'

'Well. It's been real fine talking to you brother,' he said, 'but a new skull's peering over the side here—' And he showed me the crest of his back and a jawlump like a ripple on chrome. 'Consider me gone from now on I think, okay?'

'You got it.'

The forehead dashboard topped everything.

'Like this we become men against nature,' he said, signing off.

Skilful, I thought, instead of wise.

'What d'you think?' asked John Satan, looking up from the card game. 'Empty Fred paid dear for your sins eh?'

'Maybe it's appropriate, I dunno.'

'What, think you're above it all?'

'No, no. I'm just not dark door material.'

'Deeper and deeper the hunger pleases,' clanged the Reaper, looking up.

'Indeed,' I said, itching to go, 'yes it does. Well, I have to—'

'Tell me the story of wonder,' it continued. 'Of enchantments nabbed, balloon-trousered princes, convict voyages, expensive wounds, dogs wearing lipstick, sacrifice.'

'Ay? Oh the thing I told old fish-chops here? Oh that

was ages ago.' But they insisted, and I strained to remember what the hell I'd said before. 'Well it all started,' I said, 'when.'

'Yes?' asked the devil pointedly.

And I was running, oh my brothers. Erupted out of the mirror into a restaurant and proceeded to fry and frighten the life out of everyone – hot sparks sputtered out of blackened remains indistinct at corner tables, screams, cordite and a general sense of event – police and ambulance, trouble. It's all vague in my mind.

Eddie had sold the mirror to this establishment for a fiver and was chuffed until I turned up at his place in burnt rags.

'Had a late night have we?'

'I suggest you raise your guard Eddie.'

'Oh we are delirious aren't we.'

And I thought to myself wily like, you're roaring off in a fuckin' ambulance.

The car I torched did result in a trial, by the way. Carnival it was, almost exactly like the nightmare I used to have. Judge seeking to overwhelm me with whoever he thought he was. I was so bored I started chiming like a clock – a big grandfather one in the dim light of a rarely dusted ancestral hallway. That started to put the frighteners on them. But the master stroke, as they say, was when I pounced on the jury and started raking my nails through their eyes. I was the life of the show. You should have been there. They didn't see it that way of course – many never saw again.

Trouble with the interviewer

'Then what did you do?'

'Put on my armour and went on holiday.'

'And that's as near to a conclusion as I'll be getting is it you time-wasting bastard? I've had vital things to do for the past four hours.'

'You never told me.'

'Oh God I know I never did. Oh God.'

'You're not very well are you? And you'll be a grey and gawping corpse before I desire a job here.'

'What?'

'Oh have we been talking at cross-purposes?'

'Oh my God.'

'There, there.'

'I'm just a small man.'

'I know, it's difficult. Well I have to go now.'

'But . . . but—'

'You have a question?'

'You're mad.'

'A question?'

'D'you consider it normal – I said normal – to have these monsters, these core creatures as you call them, roaring out of the wall and dragging your colleagues off to some convolute hell?'

'I consider it a blessing,' I said and walked out, laughing till my gums bled.

Of course since Fred's damnation I'd done a deal with the devil whereby he'd pop up for an occasional cameo in the nightmares I was organising for various troubled and conscience-stricken bastards. No money in it but a lotta laughs.

And also there was the Mayor's terrifying campaign – my involvement had begun when a dead wound folded my home, swallowing sofas and snapping chairs with bangs which sounded louder than they were. I was outside in a minute, watching the small contortions from the yard. The Mayor came by and said I looked angry. 'No,' I said, 'just chewing some trash and had the procedure interrupted by some grim miracle. Look.'

And I pointed at the chimney, which was developing a chin.

'It lacks grace,' he said, distracted, and moved on to the business at hand. 'I can't stand you and I'm here because I need your help in understanding why there is a law against my killing you for that reason alone.'

'Can't help you,' I said, and ran. He caught up with me, belted me a few times and then asked my advice re the media. I was happy to tell him, at first. But now, what with this and the devil I felt I needed some sort of guidance as to the next big thing in my disastrous life.

'Fry *that* and sell it over the counter brother. Do that and I'll grant you respect. Respect and more. But at this moment—'

'Now hold on a minute—'

'Oh hold on a minute he says with his fine fainting-dead-away charm. Your crouched-to-spring intellect'll have your potentially sweet and rosy life on the ropes brother and I'll be there putting money on the other side so I will. Damn you, damn you, damn you to hell!'

'Well, thank you padre I've – I've enjoyed this little . . . this talk.'

And I stumbled out of the confessional like a blinded man.

Sky the colour of beer, my past muffled in my coatpockets. Storm scaffolds in volcanic wind. What could I do but frighten a night with goat angels and apparatus? How did others make a living? Filling out the beliefs of patients. Appearing fat as usual on the gangplank, dummies in the front row to make up the numbers. Scarring the lectern with dances.

Travel agent – hammer flat the idea that adventures are accompanied by vomiting and you're on to something.

Chef? 'We found a great number of serpents in the cake.' And that's the end of that.

Dread's the same uniformed.

And I thought about my aunt and her malevolent art. 'The twelve eyes are merely decorative,' she said. This was years after her ash-head obsession, or fever. She was now making multi-generational flesh sculptures from dead wrens and lampreys. The whole thing was so unsuccessful I almost had to tell her – pieces fell off as I watched. No I thought, an artist's life is not for me. Change horses or get carried away to these extremes? Look where ash-heads got me. This was the last thing I needed in m'darkness.

'It's good auntie.'

'That's eight quid.'

'For looking.'

'Correct.'

'Well.'

So was that the way?

Snow crumping underfoot. And I saw to my right that Carver was sat on a park bench – rare to see him at large. Live-wire once. Go about clubbing people and was very influential. No one could believe it when he changed. 'There's old Carver who rode cattle,' they'd say with a sadness which was understood. And he was waving me over.

'Oho Carver,' I said.

'Oho.'

Dispossessed zoo cranes eyed us, scrawny and ricketed.

'Gutted I am, about Fred.'

'Yes,' I said, surprised at his coherence. 'Er, saw him below though, forging on.'

'How much do you know about ancient history?'

'The sky was not a spud.'

'And that's it, is it? All right. I'll cut right down to the bone and tell you something. The past becomes holy. You could troll a snowplough through the paperwork regarding my crimes. But extortion was so traditional at that time it became boring and was done grudgingly like hymns. Obscene dissipations and accomplished fencing were considered a virtue but I questioned that wisdom. Thought I of all people would find the sly way. Duck a handshake and black eye to the bodyguard.

'Innocent expectations. Leave my dent in the confidence of dominators. Ah subterfuge – only a fool would try to live without it. Many ghosts have to take the bones of idiots in order to move around, expressing themselves from behind a mask of bone and shrieking their demands, which are usually quite boring – particular kinds of biscuits and so on – jokes and biscuits are all the rage in the underworld, as you know.

'Seek nothing but yelling jokers and damaged psychology and you shall find brother. Quickly enough I learnt the language of hens and began shouting at them about the world and what they could find in it if they only thought beyond grain and the nonsense that seemed to fascinate them. No response. Return to the world, they seemed to be saying, and tell it we are happy here. After all, there aren't any fierce opponents. Right, I thought, stamping out of the farmyard, wait till you see the axe screaming toward you – and as I completed the thought, I was run over very slowly by a tractor. And the apoplectic farmer gave me one minute to run.

'That was his word – run. Voice of the community. Believe me I ran when I saw the fire and forks. Hid in a haystack, befriended a blind man who didn't know my evil, the whole nine yards. Finally got a job as a magistrate as they thought I was too ugly even to pay a whore and might thus be a credit to the legal profession.'

'I never knew that.'

'Oh yes. But I made a remark once which was my undoing, during a particularly well-publicised trial.'

'What did you say?'

' "My stomach is a large sack for kittens." '

'I see.'

'Opened a nerve store. Bastards would enter and order items I never heard of, breaking wind in time with each syllable. This is the sort of harassment I had to endure till I put my foot down on the head of a dog and said I'd "let him have it" if they didn't back off. Was there some reason they expected me to laugh at their antics with my own life?

'Angels fell in a storm of hail, bouncing. Heavy weapons

finally. Attempting re-entry, sanity broke its nails on my braincase. Raving – reruns diabolical and thought satellites, you know. Defects pellucid, head public, theoretical families in my flask. Roses in despair stop, memory feeds among rubbish. Sign here say the leaves. A pillar of salt is something to be brother. I eat gods. Gods in batter. I presume you do too?'

I was stuck for an answer.

Another silver chill crept like a ghost and he stood all feathers. 'We'll say no more about it. Except this – you, more than any other man, can save western civilisation from yourself.'

'What? Where you going?'

'Stuttering break.'

And he was walking away. England a fleeced land under clouds. Bake me that I said, pointing grand at the cliffs of Dover – and leave it too long in the fucking oven.

A lotta poltergeist activity attended the Mayor's campaign but when that had settled down we were balmy and swell. 'This can't go on forever,' I said to the Mayor, swigging brandy and counting wads of cash as thick as a dog's ear.

'Not with you involved it can't,' he replied, puffing on a cigar and, reaching idly to draw on a bell-pull, summoned a squad of bullnecked bastards to throw me out.

'Not to worry brother,' Eddie claimed later in the bar. 'They're all philanderers and fondlers of cows. Masonic bastards up to their knees in blood and spunk of an evening. You're best out of it.'

'I suppose you're correct in every detail for once Eddie,' I sighed. 'After all I've my reputation to think of.'

'That of a fawning accomplice you mean.'

And I punched out so fast he hadn't time to lower his

glass. Shrapnel everywhere. The usual lank and pointless tussle with the man whose anger's already spent and a crowd around the victim who's already the victim. But here the problem developed when Eddie began giving birth to something which was tailed and distinctly not human.

Our fear had a primal quality which put us laughing in the gutter.

Visited Eddie in the hospital. 'Why sit blear and dim indoors brother? There's a whole world out there with your name on it.'

'Why?' he asked. 'When you know something's in that crib even now learning to wreck and blame.'

'That's not the correct attitude,' I snorted. Then I took a look at the infant, its fluted nozzle and copper surface pipes. 'Eddie this isn't a child – not the way you mean. This is baby corporate, blue-collar cyborg, a core creature.'

'Look this morning I have a bad arm – the truth?'

'I'm telling you the truth Eddie – look.' And I tipped the crib at him. 'See the pump valves and gouting steam? Wise up will you, surge-gates run the bone. I suspected as much when you gave birth and weren't a woman. And it's wearing a wig.' I snatched the blonde wig from the infant and tossed it to Eddie. 'How long you been resting here?'

'Three days.'

'You're never paying.'

Eddie's silence told me he was.

'That explains it – get your things on brother, you've been had, you're out of here. Unbelievable.'

Took the creature apart at home – hydraulics and needle-teeth in the sub-etheric meat, shell-panels like a crab, the works. And this one actually contained a telescopic sight.

Meanwhile, blind with nineteen murders, the Mayor slithered into an alley and wrung his hands, seeing red. 'I'm unusual,' he grieved, 'but not unique.' He stood beneath a lamp too modern to make a romantic shadow. 'What must I *do*, finally?' His hands were becoming hammers.

Trouble with the press

'Any questions?'

'What colour was the devil's hair, what style.'

'He had no hair – if you recall, I stated he was like a fish, on its haunches.'

'Will Eddie try for another child.'

'I don't know.'

'Does Minotaur have horns.'

'Yes, two – one on his nose, one at the centre of his brow. He's large and heavily armoured.'

'Has anyone ever surpassed your girl Ruby for sheer raw power.'

'Not at all.'

'Are we to understand that the Mayor was a monster, swollen with evil.'

'Yes indeed. Proper challenge for crosshairs that one.'

'Do you consider the campaign a success.'

'Well it ended in haranguing carnage. But on the other hand here we all are, talking about it. I should add that the Mayor called me back to the campaign for today's conference because he himself is stricken with a flesh malady, a result of prolonged exposure to infant core creatures.'

'Did the Mayor manufacture the implant which grew in Eddie.'

'It's unclear, the premise of his research. Midbrain standardisation and transformation parties were the rage. You know – victim invited unawares, core creatures erupting in his head, splintering blue eyes, gentlemen observe, a parasol shields all. The Mayor considered this entertainment. But molecularly he has begun to grow metal-metal bonds and produce a polymetal alloy with rhodium indicated on the carbon.'

'Are you claiming the Mayor's monatomic elements are orbitally rearranged?'

'Yes I am.'

'Has this been verified by thermogravimetric analysis?'

'That's right, and he never volatised.'

'Was this witnessed by anyone sane?'

'No it wasn't.'

Unease amid the crowd.

'In addition there was a fifty-six per cent weight base on a silica test boat.'

'You're claiming a Hudson fifty-six per cent variable?'

'I am.'

At this the hacks began standing affronted, yelling abuse, throwing trash. 'Fraud!' was the accusation which cut the deepest brother. And I was scarpering.

Bakery was the safest place to hide – the dough would actually change shape and conform to my body shape, if I caught it early. 'How are you?' muttered the baker, drawing me out of the oven, though he was not really interested.

'Passably scorched.'

'You were not so clever when you entered the furnace,' he sneered.

Next day the story was flagged by the headline EXPOSED – THE LEAN CHICKEN MEAT WITHIN THE NEWLY SAWN ELM.

And that was the end of my short term in the spotlight. Tradewinds blew through the library, disturbing the flaked skin of Minotaur's forehead. 'I can't believe this is what I've come to,' he said, leaning my way and pointing vaguely at the drifting curtains. Ship spars were propped against the wall as if someone here had the wherewithal to use them. Beercans and sealife. Also a worn carved figurehead of a woman, which would shout in a guttural foreign language just when we least expected it. Among the things we needed, this was the last.

'These facts,' I told him, without moving, 'do not depend on, nor have an awareness of, your beliefs.'

'You and whose army?' he yelled, then looked immediately abashed at his own remark. 'Sorry,' he muttered, his coastline mouth clumping shut.

Bob entered, thundering. 'How did you bastards get in here?'

'Through the mirror,' I said, without looking up.

'Don't you understand there's a time and place for that?' he gasped. 'Minotaur knows – don't you?'

'It's true, actually. Knew someone who abused it like this – excursion to wars and his equilibrium took off, started seeing a crust of moments on the wall, phosphene and scrambling.'

'What happened to him?'

'Millionaire.'

'You're not helping,' shouted Bob to Minotaur, and stormed to the window, tossing the curtains aside – he pointed across the water to a slice of city. 'That place doesn't exist yet, what the hell do you think you're playing at?'

'Simmer down brother,' said Minotaur. 'We haven't interfered. We've not moved from these chairs for three days, precisely because of the havoc we might wreak upon the continuum.' In fact we just couldn't be arsed to get up or do anything but it sounded mature. 'All's well, now sit down and get your choppers round these little beauties.'

Minotaur bit the head off a fish and threw the body aside. There were thousands of similar bodies on the library floor.

'Hang on how many of these mothers have you been eating?' Bob asked, aghast.

'As many as you can see brother.'

'In three days?'

'Each day.'

'Oh come on,' I piped up at Bob, 'they're only trout.'

'Trout? These are bowfin you moron.'

'Eh?'

'Bowfin.' Bob stared back and forth between me and Minotaur. 'You don't get the significance of your actions do you, not really. Look at this.' He picked up one of the creatures and gestured at it. 'Rounded gob, sail fin along dorsal, stumpy arse, and the young ones' – and he discarded the adult three-footer for an infant – 'have this weird clinging organ on the tip of the snout by which they attach themselves to aquatic plants. That sound like anyone you know?'

'What's the big deal brother?' said Minotaur.

'I think I understand what he's getting at brother,' I said, retrieving one of the uneaten bowfin and staring it in the face. I pressed the gill release and the mouth gupped open. 'They look exactly like Eddie.'

'Eh?' And Minotaur spat the head out, examining the mashed remains. 'Oh my God.'

'Yes gentlemen,' said Bob with irony, and sat into the deeps of an armchair. 'Even its behaviour. Usually seen motionless and blankly staring, yards from the action. Retains primitive features, including an air bladder which enables it to live in stagnant swamps and, yes, even out of water for a while.'

'Fish out of water,' chuckled Minotaur grimly. 'Makes perfect sense.'

'I've always thought he resembled a sort of frog, eh,' I muttered pensively.

'One of evolution's dark dead-ends perhaps,' said Bob, 'all stink and soggy cardboard.'

'With gubby lips over which lies spill like rainwater from a gutter gargoyle.'

'His sanity ritually burnt in sacrifice to blowheaded visitants only he can see.'

'Pointed to a danger behind me,' said Minotaur, gulping beer from a can, 'and made off with treasures while I turned.'

'Goes without blinking for hours then fifty at once,' I said.

'The almost featureless coinage of that man's character clips this world like a skimming stone.'

'Oh yes, he's ferociously lethargic, wilfully unfinished, classically mad.'

'A failure for whom we make constant and pitying allowances.'

'Pathetically pissed-up and pretending otherwise.'

'Sweats like a kettle when thinking of the future.'

‘Says he never dreams but shrieks before dawn.’
‘In curlers all day and eyes in a jar.’
‘No mind, beacon for academe.’
‘Pounded jellyfish with heavy stone.’
‘That’s when his mother knew he was a bad ’un.’
‘Wet behind the heart.’
‘Unashamed and dull.’
‘Mock tears, permanent and crywolf.’
‘Promises shattered, debts forgotten.’
‘Doubt all, believe nothing.’
‘Wrecks the match with Kraut melodies.’
‘Click of a bone when he raises the pint.’
‘Says he knows horses and I bet he does.’
‘Plays the piano and won’t admit it.’
‘Boiling blush when you mention cattle.’
‘Falls on the ground when you punch his face.’
‘Beckons kittens into horror.’
‘Snips off the tongues of sparrow chicks.’
‘Upper storey of his courage.’
‘Whacked to climax with a bible belt.’
‘Forbidden delights of antlered skull.’
‘New cement floor in basement.’
‘Bell jar in kitchen.’
‘Magnifying glass in toilet.’
‘Murder between meals.’
‘Birds’ underwear.’
‘Eats dogfood.’
‘Eats dogs.’
‘Money and no job.’
‘Death and no body.’
‘Sex and no women.’
‘Cuttlefish and no parrot.’
‘Grew green beard.’

'There's horror, brothers.'
'Cheers.'

Trouble with Eddie

'More than I . . .'

'What was that Eddie?'

'No more. This is more than I can take you bastard. You *bastard* more than one or any man can take.'

'You all right Eddie?'

'After . . . *this* am I all right?'

'Don't follow you.'

'Hours. Five hours I listen to this. This and more, coughing back at me every slander you've ever dealt out eh? My own words too, twisted, yes twisted to fit your attitude. Candy to a babe. By Christ I'll tear out everything you've got through your smug face.'

'Not you.'

'You think you'll escape the consequences forever.'

'We had a deal here brother, eh?'

'Like some tankard-clashing reveller.'

'Did we or did we not have a deal? I could tell it in my own sweet way. Minotaur, Bob, Ruby, Satan, election run by pteranadon in cupboard, everything.'

'What about a pteranadon?'

'Pteranadon. Leatherwinged bastard. Head like a U-boat.'

'You mean a dinosaur.'

'Woken up at last have we? Yes Sonny Jim a dinosaur – thought that'd get your obscene ears flapping.'

'*What's* obscene about me ears?'

'Come on I've been over this – the pteranadon was banged up for malfeasance of club moneys, right? Spent it all on death and bloody murder.'

And Eddie was overturning the table and making a few preliminary jabs with the knife. The bar was empty except for the barman, who was sat reading a tattered book about nerve endings. So I only had the old charm to protect me.

'Where are you heading Eddie? Years pass. Radio advice aids your choice of shrub and you're an old man. Oh, yes – breakfast exhibits brought by a nurse if you're lucky.'

Eddie thrashed aside a load of chairs and advanced.

'And what are your memories. Traffic forms a bitter smile, dogs ink the path, love is rejected. A cloakroom stub and grey shudder – there's your finest hour.'

Eddie slashed wildly to left and right as I dodged backward and skirted the tables.

'Massive devaluation Eddie. A pinball ding your death-knell. Stranger stands over you, living world with a spade. You'll be black and blowing methane before anyone misses you.'

Eddie lunged and I ducked aside so the dagger punctured the wheezing rubber belly above the fireplace. The barman glanced up. 'Simmer down lads – and don't be damaging that wheezing rubber belly there now, people come from miles around to see it in action.'

'You're halfway there Eddie,' I continued, gasping with

exertion. 'Oh yes I see it in your stare. Like a bowfin drying on a harbour wall.'

'Bastard!' he screamed, and threw himself headfirst at me.

'And your hair's all wrong,' I added, though I doubt he heard me through the din of my various bones exploding.

In a while the wall-hung ornamental trilobites began fiddling their legs. Time to go. The barman unlocked and let us out to a street devoid of grave-fillers. England a birthmark on the flying world. What possible impudence suffices.

Breezes lapped me like a cat. Eddie buttoned his coat to the throat. 'So that stuff about the world and all,' he said, 'is that really the way of it d'you reckon?'

'Sure Eddie. Time your obstacles and collide well – life is suffering. Leadership the balcony, homicide the ladder. I'll be seeing you then.'

'Oh yes sure I'll see you,' he said, vague. Instantly he tripped and fell into a load of nettles. Left him there, shaking my head.

So how did Eddie end?

Loafing a failure at the table?

Feeding his eyes on climbs of fields from a dungeon window?

Riding his cloak in huge winds?

Gnashing cigars in smokelaze and stabbing cards at a table?

Riding confusion to the army, caterpillar fists curving corners on flagday?

An extravagant death on the roof of the world?

Stumbling after the lost and damned, a buccaneer to nowhere in deserts of uniform?

Alone with the skeleton of a sandwich and his deal with dread?

Drugshop eyes all pause, hours enchanted, answering one thing forever?

Asleep in the rising moon to know that strange glory?

Chairsad in soupmanners?

Onward in poison?

Divine to the gallows?

Inflammatory bullshit fuelled speculation that Eddie was off his rocker. Assailed by creditors and theological doubt, he spent two years cultivating hernias in a hydroponic glasshouse nursery, funnelling his guilt and fear into a lifestyle of dissipation and gaudy excess. The same year he was photographed body-surfing on the north shore of Oahu Island – visual enhancement showed a spooky chihuahua perched on his left shoulder.

He was arrested for attaching a squid to the face of a mime near Paris's Pompidou Centre. He served a year, during which time he built a tin effigy of a snarling midget.

He travelled the States, financing his lusts with a series of odd jobs including those of a Mexican, a snail, a bartender and a freelance harbinger of death, finally becoming a force to be reckoned with in the white slave trade. The following year he was attacked by an enraged chimp and shot it dead with a pistol, angering the masses and setting the seal upon his reputation as a charming man. The capper to his media profile was a catchphrase philosophy: 'Society? Sleep in it, fat and radical.'

Eddie gave a lecture to a bunch of school kids as to how his life had been wrecked by the simple inability to differentiate food from garbage. By delineating each of his mistakes he left a clear trail for them to follow if they wanted to be like him – sun-bronzed, respected and paid by the truckload to talk this crap at a public venue. Then he bit the head off a live hen and spat it at the front row, where the blank faces of the organisers received it like a sacrament.

He appeared on talk shows, laughing at nothing. He endorsed a brand of bait. During a radio slot, suggestions poured in as to how his face could be remoulded in a more realistic fashion – some said the whole snout area should be removed and replaced with a human nose. That made Eddie so angry he cursed the material world on air, storming off to questing and amazon divinity.

Myself I didn't hear from Eddie for years, by which time I was due to be sacrificed on an immense platform powdered in snow. I won't waste time explaining my crime or subsequent escape – suffice it to say both required a certain clean-burning arrogance. (I'd been having a lot of bad luck since Eddie made good. Earpopping roofdives, exploding glass, misfiring airbags, tides of snot, panic jackets, plain vans, inexplicable things.)

Anyway the execution proceeded after some berating torture. All the usual ceremony, masks, broad cutlasses a-tasselled with silk and so on – until I stood and told them I had to go for a slash and all hell broke loose. 'Transgressor!' they were screaming, and I smiled. Didn't know it was meant to be derogatory. We all have moments like this I suppose, when the run of things is re-established and the pain courses through our veins again like the love of an adored one.

The clock struck twelve, scholars urged me to look damned.

'I can hear election arms breaking,' I said – I thought this was the way but oh no. Once again I'd diverged from the approved and unwritten text. Nemesis crush – one at a time please.

So now I was boasting about the fact that I actually had no body contents – solid skin you understand, like an undifferentiated flesh statue – when I saw that the person beheaded in the queue before me didn't have any detail either – the neck stump looked like a bitten-down milk lolly or something, creamy white and no detail. There's the longterm effect of being your own man, I thought. Save the charm and outward signs for your mother.

Stop everything – urgent fax. Blade halted in the air. And some cossack rider comes up with a flap of paper.

The first second and third map only included the surface of the land but the next, hidden under a paving in the cellar, showed everything in detail. There was flooding in most of the cathedrals but the ones made of gold were mostly all right. Yours truly,
eddie.

There's the only word in five years – you can see why I was bored and tried to fry every memory I had of the bastard.

Let the floor hug my side. I'm slapping like a flounder. My kidneys have stopped beating and my head is against the grate. I reach through emerald-empty bottles. My resentment has a valve I can barely reach around. I'm nearly thirty and every bastard on earth knows where I am.

Ladies and gentlemen, there will come a time when you'll thank me.